Train Whistle
Guitar

Also by ALBERT MURRAY

THE OMNI-AMERICANS
SOUTH TO A VERY OLD PLACE
THE HERO AND THE BLUES

Train Whistle Guitar

Albert Murray

McGRAW-HILL BOOK COMPANY
New York / St. Louis / San Francisco / Toronto

PS
3563
.U764
T7
1974

Library of Congress Cataloging in Publication Data

Murray, Albert.
    Trainwhistle guitar.

    I. Title.
PZ4.M97917Tr   [PS3563.U764]   813'.5'4   73–20086
ISBN 0–07–044087–5

for
MICHELE

There was a chinaberry tree in the front yard of that house in those days, and in early spring the showers outside that window always used to become pale green again. Then before long there would be chinaberry blossoms. Then it would be maytime and then junebugtime and no more school bell mornings until next September, and when you came out onto the front porch and it was fair there were chinaberry shadows on the swing and the rocking chair, and chinaberry shade all the way from the steps to the gate.

When you climbed up to the best place in the china-berry tree and looked out across Gins Alley during that time of the year the kite pasture, through which you took the short cut to the post office, would be a meadow of dog fennels again. So there would also be jimson weeds as well as ragworts and rabbit tobacco along the curving roadside from the sweet gum corner to the pump shed, and poke-salad from there to the AT & N.

You couldn't see the post office flag from the chinaberry tree because it was down in Buckshaw Flat at the L & N whistlestop. You couldn't see the switch sidings for the sawmills along that part of Mobile River either, because all that was on the other side of the tank yard of the Gulf Refining Company. All you could see beyond the kite pasture were the telegraph poles and the sky above the pine ridge overlooking Chickasabogue Creek and Hog Bayou.

You couldn't see the blackberry slopes near the L & N Section Gang Quarters because first there were the honeysuckle thickets and then Skin Game Jungle where the best muscadine vines were and in which there were also some of the same owl tree holes you knew about from fireside ghost stories about treasures buried by the pirates and the Confederates.

Southeast of all of that was the L & N clearing, across which you could see the trains and beyond which you could also see that part of the river. Next on the horizon due south was Three Mile Crest, which blocked off Dodge Mill Bottom and that part of Three Mile Creek. So you couldn't see the waterfront either, nor any part of the downtown Mobile, Alabama skyline, not even with real binoculars.

Nor could you see One Mile Bridge beyond the treeline to the southwest. Nor the pecan orchard which you knew was due west looking out over the gate and the sunflowers and across the AT & N cut, which you couldn't see either. Nor African Baptist Hill. But between that neighborhood and the Chickasaw Highway was the Southern Railroad, whose night whistles you could sometimes hear as sometimes after midnight you could also hear the M & O, the

GM & O and the GM & N en route to St. Louis, Missouri and Kansas City by way of Meridian, Mississippi.

All you could see due north up Dodge Mill Road beyond Buckshaw Corner and the crawfish pond that was once part of a Civil War artillery embankment was the sky above Bay Poplar Woods fading away into the marco polo blue horizon mist on the other side of which were such express train destinations as Birmingham, Alabama and Nashville, Tennessee, and Cincinnati, Ohio, and Detroit, Michigan, plus the snowbound Klondike of Canada plus the icebound tundras of Alaska plus the North Pole.

The Official name of that place (which is perhaps even more of a location in time than an intersection on a map) was Gasoline Point, Alabama, because that was what our post office address was, and it was also the name on the L & N timetable and the road map. But once upon a time it was also the briarpatch, which is why my nickname was then Scooter, and is also why the chinaberry tree (that was ever as tall as any fairy tale beanstalk) was, among other things, my spyglass tree.

I used to say My name is also Jack the Rabbit because my home is in the briarpatch, and Little Buddy (than whom there was never a better riddle buddy) used to say Me my name is Jack the Rabbit also because my home is also in the also and also of the briarpatch because that is also where I was also bred and also born. And when I also used to say My name is also Jack the Bear he always used to say My home is also nowhere and also anywhere and also everywhere.

Because the also and also of all of that was also the also plus also of so many of the twelve-bar twelve-string guitar riddles you got whether in idiomatic iambics or otherwise mostly from Luzana Cholly who was the one who used to walk his trochaic-sporty stomping-ground limp-walk picking and plucking and knuckle knocking and strumming (like an anapestic locomotive) while singsongsaying Anywhere I hang my hat anywhere I prop my feet. Who could drink muddy water who could sleep in a hollow log.

The color you almost always remember when you remember Little Buddy Marshall is sky-blue. Because that shimmering summer sunshine blueness in which neighborhood hens used to cackle while distant yard dogs used to bark and mosquito hawks used to flit and float along nearby barbwire fences, was a boy's color. Because such blueness also meant that it was whistling time and rambling time. And also baseball time. Because that silver bright midafternoon sky above outfields was the main thing Little Buddy Marshall and I were almost always most likely to be wishing for back in those days when we used to make up our own dirty verses for that old song about it ain't gonna rain no more no more.

But the shade of blue and blueness you always remem-

6

ber whenever and for whatever reason you remember Luzana Cholly is steel blue, which is also the clean, oil-smelling
color of gunmetal and the gray-purple patina of freight train
engines and railroad slag. Because in those days, that was a
man's color (even as tobacco plus black coffee was a man's
smell), and Luzana Cholly also carried a blue steel .32-20 on
a .44 frame in his underarm holster. His face and hands
were leather brown like dark rawhide. But blue steel is the
color you always remember when you remember how his
guitar used to sound.

Sometimes he used to smell like coffee plus Prince Albert cigarettes, which he rolled himself, and sometimes it
was a White Owl Cigar, and sometimes it was Brown's
Mule Chewing Tobacco. But when he was wearing slick
starched wash-faded blue denim overalls plus tucked in
jumper plus his black and white houndstooth-checked cap
plus high top, glove-soft banker-style Stacey Adams, which
was what he almost always traveled in, he also smelled
like green oak steam. And when he was dressed up in his
tailor-made black broadcloth boxback plus pegtop hickory-
striped pants plus either a silk candy-striped or silk pongee
shirt plus knitted tie and diamond stickpin plus an always
brand new gingerly blocked black John B. Stetson hat because he was on his way somewhere either to gamble or to
play his guitar, what he smelled like was barbershop talcum
and crisp new folding money.

I can remember being aware of Luzana Cholly all the
way back there in the blue meshes of that wee winking
blinking and nod web of bedtime story time when I couldn't
yet follow the thread of the yarns I was to realize later on
that somebody was forever spinning about something he
had done, back when all of that was mainly grown folks
talking among themselves by the fireside or on the swingporch as if you were not even there: saying Luzana and

7

old Luzana and old Luze, and I didn't know what, to say nothing of where Louisiana was.

But I already knew who he himself was even then, and I could see him very clearly whenever they said his name because I still can't remember any point in time when I had not already seen him coming up that road from around the bend and down in the L & N railroad bottom. Nor can I remember when I had not yet heard him playing the blues on his guitar as if he were also an engineer telling tall tales on a train whistle, his left hand doing most of the talking including the laughing and signifying as well as the moaning and crying and even the whining, while his right hand thumped the wheels going somewhere.

Then there was also his notorious holler, the sound of which was always far away and long coming as if from somewhere way down under. Most of the time (but not always) it started low like it was going to be a moan or even a song, and then it jumped all the way to the very top of his voice and suddenly broke off. Then it came back, and this time it was already at the top. Then as often as not he would make three or four, or sometimes three followed by four, bark-like squalls and let it die away in the darkness (you remember it mostly as a nighttime sound); and Mama always used to say he was whooping and hollering like somebody back on the old plantations and back in the old turpentine woods, and one time Papa said maybe so but it was more like one of them old Luzana swamp hollers the Cajuns did in the shrimp bayous. But I myself always thought of it as being something else that was like a train, a bad express train saying Look out this me and here I come and I'm coming through one more time.

I knew that much about Luzana Cholly even before I was big enough to climb the chinaberry tree. Then finally I could climb all the way to the top, and I also knew how to box the compass; so I also knew what Louisiana was as well as where, or at least which way, it was from where I was.

At first he was somebody I used to see and hear playing the guitar when he was back in town once more. I hadn't yet found out very much about him. Nor was I ever to find out very much that can actually be documented. But it is as if I have always known that he was as rough and ready as rawhide and as hard and weather worthy as blue steel, and that he was always either going somewhere or coming back from somewhere and that he had the best walk in the world, barring none (until Stagolee Dupas (*fils*) came to town).

Anyway I had already learned to do my version of that walk and was doing the stew out of it long before Little Buddy Marshall first saw it, because he probably saw me doing it and asked me about it before he saw Luzana Cholly himself and that is probably how he found out about Luzana Cholly and rawhide and blue steel in the first place.

During that time before Little Buddy came was also when I was first called Mister. Miss Tee, who was the one I had always regarded as being without doubt the best of all Big Auntees, had always called me My Mister; and Mama had always called me Little Man and My Little Man and Mama's Little Man; but some time after Little Buddy Marshall came she used to drop the *Little* part off and that is how they started calling me Mister Man before my nickname became Scooter. But long before Little Buddy Marshall came I had been telling myself that Luzana Cholly was the Man I wanted to be like.

Then Little Buddy Marshall was there and it was as if time itself were sky-blue; and every day was for whistling secret signals and going somewhere to do something you had to have nerves as strong as rawhide to get away with. Luzana Cholly was the one we always used to try to do everything

9

like in those days. Even when you were about to do something that had nothing whatsoever to do with anything you had ever heard about him, as often as not when your turn came you said Watch old Luze. Here come old Luze. This old Luze. If Luze can't ain't nobody can.

And then not only had we come to know as much as we did about what he was like when he was there in the flesh and blood, we also knew how to talk to him, because by that time he also knew who we were. Sometimes we would come upon him sitting somewhere by himself tuning and strumming his guitar and he would let us stay and listen as long as we wanted to, and sometimes he would sneak our names into some very well known ballad just to signify at us about something, and sometimes he would make up new ballads right on the spot just to tell us stories.

We found out that the best time to signify at him because you needed some spending change was when he was on his way to the Skin Game Jungles. (Also: as far as you could tell, gambling and playing the guitar and riding the rails to and from far away places were the only steady things he ever had done or ever would do, except during the time he was in the Army and the times he had been in jail—and not only had he been to jail and the county farm, he had done time in the penitentiary!)

We were supposed to bring him good luck by woofing at him when he was headed for a skin game. So most of the time we used to try to catch him late Saturday after-

noon as he came across the oil road from Gins Alley coming
from Miss Pauline Anderson's Cookshop. Sometimes he
would have his guitar slung across his back even then, and
that he was wearing his .32-20 in his underarm holster goes
without saying.

Say now hey now Mister Luzana Cholly.

Mister Luzana Cholly one time.

(Watch out because here come old Luzana goddamn
Cholly one more goddamn time and one goddamn time
more and don't give a goddamn who the hell knows it.)

Mister Luzana Cholly all night long.

Yeah me, ain't nobody else but.

*The one and only Mister Luzana Cholly from Bogalu-
zana bolly.*

(Not because he was born and raised in Bogalusa,
Louisiana; because he once told us he was bred and born in
Alabama, and was brought up here and there to root hog
or die poor. Somebody had started calling him Luzana because that was where he had just come back in town from
when he made his first reputation as a twelve-string guitar
player second to none, including Leadbelly. Then it also
kept people from confusing him with Choctaw Cholly, who
was part Indian and Chastang Cholly the Cajun.)

Got the world in a jug.

And the stopper in your hand.

Y'all tell em, 'cause I ain't got the heart.

A man among men.

And Lord God among women!

Well tell the dy ya.

He would be standing wide legged and laughing and
holding a wad of Brown's Mule Chewing Tobacco in with
his tongue at the same time. Then he skeet a spat of amber
juice to one side like some clutch hitters do when they step

up to the plate, and then he would wipe the back of his leathery hand across his mouth and squint his eyes the way some batters sight out at the pitcher's mound.

Tell the goddamn dyyyy ya! He leveled and aimed his finger and then jerked it up like a pistol firing and recoiling.

Can't tell no more though.

How come, little sooner, how the goddamn hell come?

B'cause money talks.

Well shut my mouth. Shut my big wide mouth and call me suitcase.

Ain't nobody can do that.

Not nobody that got to eat and sleep.

I knowed y'all could tell em. I always did know good and damn well y'all could tell em. And y'all done just told em.

But we ain't go'n tell no more.

We sure ain't.

Talk don't mean a thing in the world if you ain't got nothing to back it up with.

He would laugh again then and we would stand waiting because we knew he was going to run his hand deep down into his pocket and come up not with the two customary nickels but two quarters between his fingers. He would flick them into the air as if they were jacks and catch them again, one in each hand; and then he would close and cross his hand, making as if to look elsewhere, flip one to me and one to Little Buddy Marshall.

Now talk. But don't talk too loud and don't tell too much, and handle your money like the whitefolks does.

Mama used to say he was don't-carified, and Little Buddy Marshall used to call him hellfied Mister Goddamn hellfied Luzana ass-kicking Cholly; and he didn't mean hell-defying, or hell-fired either. Because you couldn't say he was hell-defying because you couldn't even say he ever really went for bad, not even when he was whooping that holler he was so notorious for. Perhaps that was *somewhat* hell-defying to some folks, but even so what it really meant as much as anything else was I don't give a goddamn if I am hell-defying, which is something nobody driven by hell fire ever had time to say.

As for going for bad, that was the last thing he needed to do, since everybody, black or white, who knew anything at all about him already knew that when he made a promise he meant if it's the last thing I do, if it's the last thing I'm able to do on this earth. Which everybody also knew meant if you cross me I'll kill you and pay for you, as much as it meant anything else. Because the idea of going to jail didn't scare him at all, and the idea of getting lynch-mobbed didn't faze him either. All I can remember him ever saying about that was: If they shoot at me they sure better not miss me they sure better get me that first time. Whitefolks used to say he was a crazy nigger, but what they really meant or should have meant was that he was confusing to them. Because if they knew him well enough to call him crazy they also had to know enough about him to realize that he wasn't foolhardy, or even careless, not even what they wanted to mean when they used to call somebody biggity. Somehow or other it was as if they respected him precisely because he didn't seem to care anything about them one way or the other. They certainly respected the fact that he wasn't going to take any foolishness off of them.

Gasoline Point folks also said he was crazy. But they meant their own meaning. Because when they said crazy they really meant something else, they meant exactly the same thing as when they called him a fool. At some point some time ago (probably when my favorite teacher was Miss Lexine Metcalf) I decided that what they were talking about was something like poetic madness, and that was their way of saying that he was forever doing something unheard of if not downright outrageous, doing the hell out of it, and not only getting away with whatever it was, but making you like it to boot. You could tell that was the way they felt by the way they almost always shook their heads laughing even as they said it, and sometimes even before they said it: Old crazy Luzana Cholly can sure play the fool out of that guitar. Old crazy Luzana Cholly is a guitar playing fool and a card playing fool and a pistol packing fool and a freight train snagging fool, and don't care who knows it.

I still cannot remember ever having heard anybody saying anything about Luzana Cholly's mother and father. Most of the time you forgot all about that part of his existence just as most people had probably long since forgotten whether they had ever heard his family name. Nobody I know ever heard him use it, and no sooner had you thought about it than you suddenly realized that he didn't seem ever to have had or to have needed any family at all. Nor did he seem to need a wife or steady woman either. But that was because he was not yet ready to quit the trail and settle down. Because he had lived with more women from time to time and place to place than the average man could or would even try to shake a stick at.

The more I think about all of that the more I realize that you never could tell which part of what you heard about something he had done had actually happened and which part somebody else had probably made up. Nor did it ever really matter which was which. Not to anybody I ever knew in Gasoline Point, Alabama, in any case, to most of whom all you had to do was mention his name and they were ready to believe any claim you made for him, the more outrageously improbable the better. All you had to do was say Luzana Cholly old Luzana Cholly old Luze. All you had to do was see that sporty limp walk. Not to mention his voice, which was as smoke-blue sounding as the Philamayork-skyline-blue mist beyond blue steel railroad bridges. Not to mention how he was forever turning guitar strings into train whistles which were not only the once-upon-a-time voices of storytellers but of all the voices saying what was being said in the stories as well.

Not that I who have always been told that I was born to be somebody did not always know on my deepest levels of comprehension that the somebody-ness of Luzana Cholly was of its very nature nothing if not legendary. Which no doubt also has something to do with why I almost always used to feel so numb and strange when somebody other than kinfolks called out the name that Mama had given me and Miss Tee had taught me how to spell and write. I always jumped, even when I didn't move. And in school I wanted to hide, but you had to answer because it was the teacher calling the roll so I said Present and it didn't sound like myself at all. It was not until Uncle Jerome nicknamed me Scooter that I could say That's me, that's who I am and what I am and what I do.

Anyway, such somehow has always been the nature of legends and legendary men (which probably exist to beget other lengends and would-be lengendary men in the first place) that every time Little Buddy Marshall and I used to do that sporty-blue limp-walk (which told the whole world that you were ready for something because at worst you had only been ever so slightly sprained and bruised by all the terrible situations you had been through) we were also reminding ourselves of the inevitability of the day when we too would have to grab ourselves an expert armful of lightning special L & N freight train rolling north by east to the steel blue castles and patent leather avenues of Philamayork, which was the lodestone center of the universe.

That is why we had started practicing freight train hopping on the tanks and boxcars in the switchyard as soon as we had gained enough leeway to sneak that far away from the neighborhood. That was the first big step, and you were already running a double risk (of being caught and of getting maimed for life at the very least) as soon as you started playing with something as forbidden as that, which was what they told you everything you had ever heard about old Peg Leg Nat to keep you from doing. Old Peg Leg Nat Carver, who had a head as bald and shiny as the nickelplated radiator of the Packard Straight Eight and who prided himself on being able to butt like a billy goat, and who now spent most of his time fishing and selling fresh fish and shrimp and crabs from the greenness of his palm frond covered wheelbarrow. Somebody was always reminding you of what had happened to him. Mama for instance, who could never pass up a chance to say Here come old Peg Leg Nat and a peg leg or something worse is just exactly what messing around with freight trains will get you. And she had had me scared for a while, but not for long. Because then Little Buddy Marshall and I found out that what had happened probably never would have happened if Old Nat, who was then known as old Butt Head Nat, had not been drunk and trying to show everybody how fancy he was. And anyway anybody could see that getting his leg cut off hadn't really stopped old Nat for good, since not only did he still do it again every time he got the itch to go somewhere, he also could still beat any two-legged man except Luzana Cholly himself snagging anything rolling through Gasoline Point.

❂

Then Little Buddy found out that Luzana Cholly himself was getting ready to leave town again soon and I myself found out which way he was going to be heading (but not where) and which day, so we also knew which train; and that was when we got everything together and started waiting.

Then at long last after all the boy blue dreaming and scheming and all the spyglass scanning it was that day and we were there in that place because it was time to take the next step. I was wearing my high top brogan shoes and I had on my corduroy pants and a sweater under my overalls with my jumper tucked in. I was also wearing my navy blue baseball cap and my rawhide wristband and I had my pitcher's glove folded fingers up in my left hip pocket. And Little Buddy was wearing and carrying the same amount of the very same traveling gear except for his thin first base pad instead of big thick Sears Roebuck catcher's mitt. Our other things plus something to eat were rolled up in our expertly tied blanket rolls so that we could maneuver with both arms free.

Little Buddy was also carrying Mister Big Buddy Marshall's pearl handled .38 Smith & Wesson. And our standard equipment for any trip outside that neighborhood in those days always included our all-purpose jackknives, which we had learned to snap open like a switchblade and could also flip like a Mexican dagger. Also, buckskin pioneers and

17

wilderness scouts that we would always be, we had not forgotten hooks and twine to fish with. Nor were we ever to be caught in any root hog or die poor situation without our trusty old Y-stock (plus inner tube rubber plus shoe tongue leather) slingshots and a drawstring Bull Durham pouch of birdshot babbitt metal plus at least a handful of peewee sized gravel pebbles.

It was May but school was not out of session yet, so not only were we running away from home we were also playing hooky, for which the Truant Officer also known as the School Police could take you to Juvenile Court and have you detained and then sent to the Reformatory School. (Mt. Meigs and Wetumpka were where they used to send you in those days. No wonder I still remember them as being two of the ugliest place names in the whole state of Alabama. Not as ugly as Bay Minette, which I still remember as a prototype of all the rattlesnake nests of rawboned hawkeyed nigger-fearing lynch-happy peckerwoods I've ever seen or heard tell of. But ugly enough to offset most of the things you didn't like about grade school.)

It was hot even for that time of year, and with that many clothes on, we were already sweating. But you had to have them, and that was the best way to carry them. There was a thin breeze coming across the railroad from the river, the marsh and Polecat Bay, but the sun was so hot and bright that the rail tracks were shimmering under the wide open sky as if it were the middle of summer.

We were waiting in the thicket under the hill between where the Dodge Mill Road came down and where the oil yard switching spurs began, and from where we were you could see up and down the clearing as far as you needed to.

I have now forgotten how long we had to stay there waiting and watching the place from where we had seen Luzana Cholly come running across the right of way to the tracks so many times. But there was nothing you could do but wait then, as we knew he was doing, probably strumming his guitar and humming to himself.

Man, I wish it would hurry up and come on, Little Buddy said all of a sudden.

Man, me too, I probably said without even having to think about it.

Man, got to get to goddamn splitting, he said and I heard his fingers touching the package of cigarettes in his bib pocket.

We were sitting on the blanket rolls with our legs crossed Indian fire circle fashion. Then he was smoking another One Eleven, holding it the way we both used to do in those days, letting it dangle from the corner of your curled lips while tilting your head to one side with one eye watching and the other squinted, like a card sharper.

Boy, goddammit, you just watch me nail the sapsucker, he said.

Man, and you just watch me.

You could smell the mid-May woods up the slope behind us then, the late late dogwoods, the early honeysuckles, and the warm earth-plus-green smell of the pre-summer undergrowth. I can't remember which birds you used to hear during each season, not like I used to; but I do remember hearing a woodpecker somewhere on a dead hollow tree among all the other bird sounds that day because I also remember thinking that woodpeckers always sounded as if they were out in the open in the very brightest part of the sunshine.

Waiting and watching, you were also aware of how damp and cool the sandy soft ground was underneath you there in the gray and green shade; and you could smell that smell too, even as the Gulf Coast states breeze blew all of the maritime odors in to you from the river and the marshlands. Little Buddy finished his cigarette and flipped the stub out into the sunshine and then sat with his back against a sapling and sucked his teeth. I looked out across the railroad to where the gulls were circling over the reeds and the water.

You know something? Goddammit, when I come back here to this here little old granny-dodging burg, boy I'm going to be a goddamn man and a goddamn half, Little Buddy said, breaking the silence again.

As before, he was talking as much to himself as to me. But I said: And don't give a goddamn who knows it. Then he said: Boy, Chicago. And I said: Man, Detroit. And he said: Man, St. Louis. And I said: And Kansas City. Then: Hey, Los Angeles. Hey, San Francisco. Hey, Denver, Colorado. Him calling one and me adding another until we had leapfrogged all the way back down to the Florida Coast Line, with him doing that old section gang chant: Say I don't know but I think I will make my home in Jacksonville (Hey big boy cain't you line em).

Then I was the one, because that is when I said: Hey, you know who the only other somebody else in the world I kinda wish was here to be going too? And little Buddy said: Old Cateye Gander. Me too. Old Big-toed Gander. Man, shit I reckon.

Man, old Gander Gallagher can steal lightning if he have to.

Man, who you telling?

Man, how about that time? You know that time getting them wheels for that go-cart. That time from Buckshaw.

Right on out from under that nightwatchman's nose, man.

And everybody know they got some peckerwoods down there subject to spray your ass with birdshot just for walking too close to that fence after dark.

Man, shit I reckon. And tell you you lucky it wasn't that other barrel, because that's the one with triple ought buckshot.

Hey man but old Luze though.

Man, you know you talking about somebody now.

Talking about somebody taking the cake.

Goddammit man, boy, just think. We going!

Me and you and old hard cutting Luze, buddy.

Boy, and then when we get back, I said that and I could see it. Coming back on that Pan American I would be carrying two leather suitcases, and have a money belt and an underarm holster for my special-made .38 Special. And I would be dressed in tailor-made clothes and hand-made shoes from London, England by way of Philamayork.

Hey Lebo, I said, thinking about all that then. How long you think it might take us to get all fixed up to come back.

Man, shoot, I don't know and don't care.

You coming back when old Luze come back?

Man, I don't know. Just so we go. Man, me I just want to go.

I didn't say anything else then. Because I was trying to think about how it was actually going to be then. Because what I had been thinking about before was how I wanted it to be. I didn't say anything else because I was thinking about myself then. And then my stomach began to feel weak and I tried to think about something else. But I couldn't. Because what I suddenly remembered as soon as I closed my eyes that time was the barbershop and them talking about baseball and boxing and women and politics with the newspapers rattling and old King Oliver's band playing "Sugarfoot Stomp" on the Victrola in Papa Gumbo's cookshop next door, and I said I want to and I don't want to but I got to, then I won't have to anymore either and if I do I will be ready.

Then I looked over at Little Buddy again, who now was lying back against the tree with his hands behind his head and his eyes closed, whose legs were crossed, and who was resting as easy as some baseball players always seem able to do before gametime even with the band hot timing the music you always keep on hearing over and over when you lose. I wondered what he was really thinking. Did he really mean it when he said he didn't know and didn't even care? You couldn't tell what he was thinking, but if you knew him as well as I did it was easy enough to see that he was not about to back out now, no matter how he was feeling about it.

So I said to myself: Goddammit if Little Buddy Marshall can go goddammit I can too because goddammit ain't nothing he can do I cain't if I want to because he might be the expert catcher but I'm the ace pitcher and he can bat on both sides but I'm the all-round infield flash and I'm the prizefighter and I'm also the swimmer.

But what I found myself thinking about again then was Mama and Papa, and that was when I suddenly realized as never before how worried and bothered and puzzled they were going to be when it was not only that many hours after school but also after dark and I still was not back home yet. So that was also when I found myself thinking about Miss Tee again. Because she was the one whose house would be the very first place I was absolutely certain Mama would go looking for me, even before asking Mister Big Buddy about Little Buddy.

Hey, Lebo.

Hey, Skebo.
Skipping city.
Man, you tell em.
Getting further.
Man, ain't no lie.
Getting long gone.
Man, ain't no dooky.

Goddammit to hell, Little Buddy said then, why don't it come on?

Son-of-a-bitch, I said.

Goddamn granny-dodging son-of-a-bitching mother-fucking motherfucker, he said lighting another One Eleven, come on here son-of-a-bitching motherfucking son-of-a-bitch.

I didn't say anything else because I didn't want him to say anything else. Then I was leaning back against my tree looking out across the sandy clearing at the sky beyond the railroad and the marsh territory again, where there were clean white pieces of clouds that looked like balled up sheets in a wash tub, and the sky itself was blue like rinse water with bluing in it; and I was thinking about Mama and Papa and Uncle Jerome and Miss Tee again, and I couldn't keep myself from hoping that it was all a dream.

That was when I heard the whistle blowing for Three Mile Creek Bridge and opened my eyes and saw Little Buddy already up and slinging his roll over his shoulder.

Hey, here that son-of-a-bitch come. Hey, come on, man.

I'm here, son, I said snatching my roll into place, Don't be worrying about me. I been ready.

The engine went by, and the whistle blew again, this time for the Chickasabogue, and we were running across the sandy crunch-spongy clearing. My ears were ringing then, and I was sweating, and my neck was hot and sticky and my pants felt as if the seat had been ripped away. There was nothing but the noise of the chugging and steaming and the smell of coal smoke, and we were running into it, and then we were climbing up the fill and running along the high bed of crosstie slag and cinders.

We were trotting along in reach of it then, that close to the um chuckchuck um chuckchuck um chuckchuckchuck, catching our breath and remembering to make sure to let at least one empty boxcar go by. Then when the next gondola came Little Buddy took the front end, and I grabbed the back. I hit the hotbox with my right foot and stepped onto the step and pulled up. The wind was in my ears then, but I knew all about that from all the practice I had had by that time. So I climbed on up the short ladder and got down on the inside, and there was old Little Buddy coming grinning back toward me.

Man, what did I tell you!

Man, did you see me lam into that sucker?

Boy, we low more nailed it.

Hey, I bet old Luze he kicking it any minute now.

Man, I'm talking about cold hanging it, man.

Boy, you know it, man, I said. But I was thinking I hope so, I hope old Luze didn't change his mind, I hope we don't have to start out all by ourselves.

Hey going, boy, Little Buddy said.

Man, I done told you!

We crawled up into the left front corner out of the wind, and there was nothing to do but wait again then. We knew that this was the northbound freight that always had to pull into the hole for Number Four once she was twelve miles out, and that was when we were supposed to get to the open boxcar.

So we got the cigarettes out and lit up, and there was nothing but the rumbling thunder-like noise the wide open gondola made then, plus the far away sound of the engine and the low rolling pony tail of gray smoke coming back. We were just sitting there then, and after we began to get used to the vibration, nothing at all was happening except being there. You couldn't even see the scenery going by.

You were just there in the hereness and nowness of that time then, and I don't think you ever really remember very much about being in situations like that except the way you felt, and all I can remember now about that part is the nothingness of doing nothing, and the feeling not of going but of being taken, as of being borne away on a bare barge or even on the bare back of a storybeast.

All you could see after we went through the smokey gray lattice-work of Chickasabogue Bridge was the now yellow blue sky and the bare floor and the sides of the heavy rumbling gondola, and the only other thing I have ever remembered is how I wished something would happen because I definitely did not want to be going anywhere at all then, and I already felt lost even though I knew good and well that I was not yet twelve miles from home. Because although Little Buddy Marshall and I had certainly been many times farther away and stayed longer, this already seemed to be farther and longer than all the other times together!

❖

Then finally you could tell it was beginning to slow down, and we stood up and started getting ready. Then it was stopping and we were ready and we climbed over the side and came down the ladder and struck out forward. We were still in the bayou country, and beyond the train-smell there was the sour-sweet snakey smell of the swampland. We were running on slag and cinders again then and with the train quiet and waiting for Number Four you could hear the double crunching of our brogans echoing through the waterlogged moss-draped cypresses.

Along there the L & N Causeway embankment was almost as high as the telegraph lines, and the poles were black with a fresh coat of creosote and there were water lilies floating on the slimy green ditch that separated the railroad right of way from the edge of the swamp. Hot-collared and hustling to get to where we estimated the empty boxcar to be, we came pumping on. And then at last we saw it and could slow down and catch our breath.

And that was when we also saw that old Luzana Cholly himself was already there. We had been so busy trying to get there that we had forgotten all about him for the time being. Not only that but this was also the part that both of us had completely forgotten to think about all along. So we hadn't even thought about what we were going to say, not to mention what he was going to say.

And there he was now standing looking down at us from the open door with an unlighted cigarette in his hand. We had already stopped without even realizing it, and suddenly everything was so quiet that you could hear your heart pounding inside your head. It was as if the spot where you were had been shut off from everything else in the world. I for my part knew exactly what was going to happen then, and I was so embarrassed that I could have sunk into the ground, because I also thought: Now he's going to call us a name. Now he just might never have anything to do with us anymore.

We were standing there not so much waiting as frozen then, and he just let us stay there and feel like two wet puppies shivering, their tails tucked between their legs. Then he lit his cigarette and finally said something.

Oh no you don't oh no you don't neither. Because it ain't like that aint like that ain't never been like that and ain't never going to be not if I can help it.

He said that as much to himself as to us, but at the same time he was shaking his head not only as if we couldn't understand him but also as if we couldn't even hear him.

Y'all know it ain't like this. I know y'all know good and well it cain't be nothing like this.

Neither one of us even moved an eye. Little Buddy didn't even dig his toe into the ground.

So this what y'all up to. Don't say a word. Don't you open your mouth.

I could have crawled into a hole. I could have sunk into a pond. I could have melted leaving only a greasy spot. I could have shriveled to nothing but an ash.

Just what y'all call y'allself doing? That's what I want to know. So tell me that. Just tell me that. Don't say a word. Don't you say one word. Don't you say a goddamn mumbling word to me. Neither one of you.

We weren't even about to make a sound.

What I got a good mind to do is whale the sawdust out of both you little crustbusters. That's what I ought to be doing right now instead of talking to somebody ain't got no better sense than that.

But he didn't move. He just stood where he was looking down.

Well, I'm a son-of-a-bitch. That's what I am. I'm a

son-of-a-bitch. I'm a thick-headed son-of-a-bitch. Hell, I musta been deaf dumb and blind to boot not to know this. Goddamn!

That was all he said then, and then he jumped down and walked us to where the side spur for the southbound trains began, and all we did was sit there near the signal box and feel terrible until Number Four had come whistling by and was gone and we heard the next freight coming south. Then what he did when it finally got there was worse than any name he could ever have called us. He wouldn't let us hop it even though it was only a short haul and pickup local that was not much more than a switch engine with more cars than usual. He waited for it to slow down for the siding and then he picked me up (as they pick you up to put you in the saddle of a pony because you're not yet big enough to reach the stirrups from the ground on your own) and put me on the front end of the first gondola, and did the same thing to Little Buddy; and then he caught the next car and came forward to where we were.

So we came slow-poking it right back toward the Chickasaboque and were back in Gasoline Point before the sawmill whistles even started blowing the hands back to work from noontime. I could hardly believe that so little time had passed. But then such is the difference between legendary time and actuality, which is to say, the time you remember and the time you measure.

We came on until the train all but stopped for Three Mile Creek Bridge, and then he hopped down and took Little Buddy off first and then me, and we followed him down the steep, stubble covered embankment and then to the place the hobos used under the bridge. He unslung the guitar and sat down and lit another cigarette and flipped the match stem into the water and watched it float away. Then he sat back and looked at us again, and then he motioned for us to sit down in front of him.

That was when we found out what we found out directly from Luzana Cholly himself about hitting the road, which he (like every fireside knee-pony uncle and shade tree uncle and tool shed uncle and barbershop uncle since Uncle Remus himself) said was a whole lot more than just a notion. He was talking in his regular matter-of-fact voice again then, so we knew he was not as exasperated with us as he had been. But as for myself I was still too scandalized to face him, and as for Little Buddy, he seldom if ever looked anybody straight in the eye anyway. Not that he was ever very likely to miss any move you made.

That time was also when Luzana Cholly told me and Little Buddy what he told us about the chain gang and the penitentiary: and as he talked, his voice uncle-calm and his facts first-hand and fresh from the getting-place, he kept reaching out every now and then to touch the guitar. But only as you stroke your pet or touch a charm, or as you finger a weapon or tool or your favorite piece of sports equipment. Because he did not play any tunes or even any chords, or make up any verse for us that day. But even so, to this day I remember what he said precisely as if it had actually been another song composed specifically for us.

Then, after he had asked us if it wasn't about time for two old roustabouts like us to eat something and the two of us had shared a can of sardines while he worked on a bite from his plug of Brown's Mule Chewing Tobacco, the main thing he wanted to talk about was going to school and learning to use your head like the smart, rich and powerful whitefolks, (nor did he or anybody else I can remember mean whitefolks in general. So far as I know the only white people he thought of as being smart were precisely those who were either rich and powerful or famous. The rest were peckerwoods, about whom you had to be careful not because they were smart but because so many of them were so mean and evil about not being smart and powerful and famous). He said the young generation was supposed to take what they were already born with and learn how to put it with everything the civil engineers and inventors and doctors and lawyers and bookkeepers had found out about the world and be the one to bring about the day the old folks had always been prophesying and praying for.

The three of us just sat looking across the water then. And then we heard the next northbound freight coming, and he stood up and got ready; and he said we could watch him but we better not try to follow him this time, and we promised, and we also promised to go to school the next morning.

So then we came back up the embankment, because the train was that close, and he stood looking at us, with the guitar slung across his back. Then he put his hands on our shoulders and looked straight down into our eyes, and you knew you had to look straight back into his, and we also knew that we were no longer supposed to be ashamed in front of him because of what we had done. He was not going to tell. And we were not going to let him down.

Make old Luze proud of you, he said then, and he was almost pleading. *Make old Luze glad to take his hat off to you some of these days. You going further than old Luze ever dreamed of. Old Luze ain't been nowhere. Old Luze don't know from nothing.*

And then the train was there and we watched him snag it and then he was waving goodbye.

Sometimes I also used to call myself Jack the Nimble and Jack the Quick, and I also used to call the chinaberry tree my candlestick; and sometimes Little Buddy used to say I got your goddamn candlestick right here and also your goddamn hickory stick right here and also your goddamn greasy pole stick right here and also your goddamn totem pole stick right here and also your goddamn telegraph telephone tell-a-woman pole stick right here.

But sometimes he also used to call his baseball bat his hickory stick, and that was when I used to say my right arm is my trickery stick. And so was my left jab. Because the also and also of Luzana Cholly (which was also to become at least in part the also and also of Stagolee Kid the piano player) was also the also and also of Jack Johnson who was by all accounts and all odds the nimblest footed quickest witted Jack of them all; who could spring six feet backwards and out of punching range from a standstill, who could salivate a Spanish fighting bull with a six-inch upper-cut, whose eyes and hands were so sharp that he could reach out and snatch flies from mid-air without crushing them.

Which is why there was a cement sack punching bag hanging heavyweight-high from the lowest branch of the chinaberry tree, plus also a narrow circle that you were supposed to stand up and step into when Little Buddy said chingaling and stay there feinting and jabbing and bobbing and weaving and hooking and crossing and sneaking combinations from the minute he said ding until he said dong.

Because when the ku klux klan got mad and put on its white robes and started burning crosses just because somebody said bring me my coffee as black and strong as Jack Johnson and my scrambled eggs all beat up like poor old Jim Jeffries, I was the one they wanted to come and lynch. I was not as black or as big as Jack Johnson and I was never going to have all of my hair shaved off, but all the same as soon as I stepped into the prize ring I was the one who had set out from Galveston, Texas, not only to see the sights of the nation and seek my fortune wherever the chances were, but also to become the undisputed champion of the world. I was the one who had had to follow Tommy Burns all the way to Sidney, Australia, to knock him out and bring back the golden belt. I was the one who was the scandal of San Francisco and Chicago and New York City. I was the talk of the town in London and the rage of Paris. And I had also fought Muira bulls in Spain and had even raced against Barney Oldfield at Sheepshead Bay, because after all I was as famous for my custombuilt sports cars as for my tailor-made suits and hand tooled shoes.

32

I had come up from the knockdown and broken off all of Steve Ketchell's front teeth at the gums with one jampole right that time in Colmar, California, not only because he was trying to doublecross me after I had agreed to take it easy for a twenty round exhibition, but also because that was my way of showing him that I knew that the newspapers were all set to declare him the undisputed champion if he would bring back old John L. Sullivan's color line, which I crossed every time I stepped into the workout circle around the punching bag.

When what you were playing was baseball the chinaberry shade was the dugout and the front porch was the grandstand and the yard was the infield and the fence was the bleachers. For homeplate Little Buddy and I sometimes used a flattened out half-gallon syrup can that was only half the width of the regulation size. Sometimes all we had was a cord ball and sometimes we had a Nickel Rock but most of the time we had a used big league regulation ball from either Reach or Spalding. (You made the cord ball yourself. You could buy a Nickel Rock or Two-bit Rock or Fifty Cent Rock at Stranahan's Store. You could buy regulation balls at the Red Brick Drug Store, which was also where the Guidebook came from.)

Sometimes I used to fake with my glove like Joe Bowman when I was hesitating because there was a runner on first base, and sometimes I also used to snap my high drop like old Eddie Morgan from Chickasaw. My famous follow-through came from George Pipgras on the sports page of the Mobile Register the year the New York Yankees won the World Series from the Pittsburgh Pirates in four straight games. But the only one you needed to be any time that you wanted to be the Jack Johnson of baseball was the same old long legged sleepy walking Elroy Augustus Gaither better known as Gus the Gator and Gator Gus who used to pitch in Chickasaw, in Whistler, in Davis Avenue Park, up in Plateau, down in Bayou La Batre and Moss Point or anywhere else anybody could get up enough money to hire him before he left Mobile for Kansas City and points north.

Because (sports page pictures and cartoons or not) there was a time when I used to think that being a money ball pitcher like old Gus the Gator was what baseball was all about: because when that was what you were, as often as not, (unless somebody was able to get up enough money to hire you for the full nine innings) you didn't even come anywhere near any game—not even the Fourth of July game or the Labor Day game—before the sixth inning. Sometimes you didn't get there until the eighth, and sometimes you didn't go until somebody sent for you.

Then with the band playing "Sundown" or "Little White Lies" or "Precious Little Thing Called Love," as if it was pleading for help, you cruised up in your sporty roadster with the top down and the motor cadillacking and parked (sometimes near the grandstand, sometimes somewhere near third base and sometimes somewhere along the foul line beyond first) and sat half looking and half listening, with your left elbow on the steering wheel and your pitching arm around your honey brown finelegged frizzly headed woman for the day, while the money men from both sides took their turns and made their bids. Not that money was always what made the difference, because sometimes you let your girl choose the side (even as old Jack

Johnson used to let his woman tell him to throw his knock-out punch any time they got ready to go home and have some fried chicken. Some fried rabbit. Some barbecue with Brunswick stew. Some pickled eels. And then do some you-know-what).

Then depending on whether it was a park or a field, you went either to the clubhouse or to the thickets and put on your own personal togs, which sometimes, depending on the occasion, were only your cap, your jockstrap, your spikes with the brass toe plate and your notorious hand tailored Number Nine shirt, with your knife-edged hard finished pants turned up one turn. Then you came back and handed your sporty silk banded leghorn straw hat to your frizzly headed woman, who of course was also the one who held your warm-up sweater while you were out on the mound, and with that many of them already watching you instead of the game you stepped into the bullpen and started limbering up.

That was when somebody was bound to say: How do he feel do he feel like throwing that thing today? Somebody and somebody else and somebody else who had spent the whole week saying: Get Scooter. We got Scooter yet? We got to get up enough to bring old Scooter in there in the clutches. Somebody better get off your ass and get busy. Because if we mess around and don't, they sure in the hell will and goodbye. I'm telling you. When that cute brownskin rascal feel like chunking that thing, goodnight, fare thee the hell well and goodbye, and don't say I didn't tell you.

Then when you were warmed up enough to make Little Buddy's mitt echo so loud that the umpire had to hold up the game until you were ready to go in because most of the crowd was now watching the bullpen anyway, you knew very well all of the old signifying was going to begin again: Uhhhh-uh!

35

Yeahhh, look like he just might feel like chunking some ball today.
So, goodbye.
Uhhhh-uh!
Goodbye, sooner.
Kiss your money goodbye.
Goodbye, money. Hello, Monday morning.

Not that you always had enough to get them, and yourself out of the hole you were forever being called into. Because not even old Gator himself could do that every time; and he, after all, was the one who was supposed to be able to go out in the bottom of the ninth with a one run lead and make the first batter pop up to right, left or center; then after waving the outfielders to the sidelines and making the second man hit to first, second, shortstop or third, strike the last batter out with two balls, one called strike plus one of his mess-merizing curves followed by his special of specials the fadeaway.

Because all you had to do was be there to see that the main thing about old Gus the Gator was not how many games he saved and how much money he won but how good he always made you feel, win, lose or draw. Because afterwards everybody always said what everybody always said: Did you see him in there? Even when he had lost: Did you see old Gus in there after them rascals? Man, cain't nobody chunk that thing like the Gator.

Being also explorers and also discoverers and also wagon train scouts as well as sea pirates and cowboys among all the other things you had to be besides being also a schoolboy, Little Buddy Marshall and I knew very well that going through Chickasabogue Swamp was an expedition in itself. That was why he was not only wearing his mackinaw and his corduroys plus his mickey cochrane catcher's cap but was also carrying Mister Big Buddy's nickel-plated pearl handled .38 Smith and Wesson again. But the smoke-blue destination that day was the shipyards at Chickasaw Bend.

I was also equipped for emergency action. I was wearing my New York Yankee pitching cap and my heavy blue sweater (which was also a pitcher's warm-up sweater) and my Sears Roebuck twills and I was carrying Uncle Jerome's bowie knife. But the reason we were playing hooky was to see them working on the ships in the dry docks again. We planned to spend the whole day finding out about all that, with the cable winches grinding, the cranes swinging and the air hammers echoing like machine guns above the oil-black pier water lapping at the pilings and then we were going to come back along the AT & N and top the day off by crossing the nightmare trestle over Bay Poplar Gorge.

The first thing we did that morning was hide the books in the cache hole we used in Buckshaw mill yard. Then we laced on our marine store campaign leggings. Then we came on along the trail that sloped down into the first part of blue poplar woods, and by the time the last school bell rang we could hardly hear it, because we were already almost one third of the way to Chickasabogue Creek.

Squinting his eyes, and curling his lips, Little Buddy who was never going to be any more of a schoolboy than he was absolutely forced to be thumbed his nose and threw a dirty salute back over his shoulder in the direction from which the bell sound came and suddenly broke into old Luzana Cholly's sporty limp walk in spite of the fact that where we were was Indian territory.

Chickasaw, Chickasaw, he said, calling it out like the L & N porter we liked best in those days, Talking about Chickasaw.

But schoolboy that I already also was even then, as faint as the bell sound was, the minute I heard it I could also feel the way I always felt and see them lining up at the flagpole; and I couldn't keep myself from knowing exactly how long it would be before the Pledge of Allegiance and the high society march would be over and Miss Lexine Metcalf would be calling my name twice and looking up before marking me tardy.

Talking about Chickasaw, Little Buddy said and looked

38

at me, and I pulled my cap all the way down square and looked straight ahead and walked rocking dicty with my shoulders rounded and my arms dangling as if I were moving along the aisle of a church and a train coach at the same time.

Oh will there be one, I said looking neither to the right nor the left.

Stand up, Little Buddy said, with his cap square too, Step down.

And give me your hand for Chickasaw Bend, Alabama, I said and held my arms out palms up and then let them fall.

Chickasaw Bend, Mobile County, Aladambama United Tits of a Milk Cow, one time, Little Buddy said.

Been long hearing tell of it.

And ain't but the one.

Oh but will there be one?

Oh stand up step up step down.

Oh whosoever will.

Let him come and give me your hand.

And give God your heart, brother.

One for Chickasaw.

I thank you, praise be, I thank you.

Two for Chickasaw Bend.

Amen Amen Amen Amen.

Hey, that's all right about your goddamn school, Little Buddy said. Hey, call us the goddamn school this time.

We got your goddamn school, I said. I got your goddamn school right here.

We followed the winding trail on down the thickly wooded slope and into the moss draped bottom, and when we came to the creek bank there was a launch putt-putting along out in the channel towing a long raft of logs downstream toward Buckshaw's boom. The Chickasabogue was well over two hundred yards wide at that point, and on the other side there was a cane brake which stretched all the way out of sight to the L & N.

You couldn't see the L & N Bridge from the skiff boat landing where we were standing then, but we knew where it was because it was also the gateway through which the Chickasabogue, which was really a tributary, flowed out into the Mobile River which led down into Mobile Bay which spread out into the Gulf of Mexico which was a part of the old Spanish Main which was the beginning of the Seven Seas.

But the direction in which we were heading was upstream, which was north meandering west, so, alert not only for water moccasins and salamanders but also for wild bo' hogs and alligators we moved on into that part of the swamp; and it was the up in the day part of the morning then, and beyond the ferns and cypress trunks there was the water wrinkling in the sunshine and the sky over the distant savannas and the bayou country was clearing from smoke gray bundles of gauze to the thin silky almost-summer blueness of midmorning.

The next traffic out in the channel was another launch going downstream with a log raft which was even longer than the first, and not far behind was a tug with a string of empty Tennessee Coal Iron Company barges. We padded softly on having a good time just being where we wanted to be and doing what we wanted to do with Chickasaw still to come. Then the first tug heading upstream came into sight behind us, and the barges behind it were loaded with rosin and tar, and turpentine.

There was a blueness which went with the odor of caulking tar and turpentine and which was to twine and tarpaulin what steel blue was to rawhide; and it went with Mobile because it was seaport blue, which was that infinite color of horizons beyond harbors and salt foam, that compass and spyglass blue against which gulls circled and soared above red clanging buoys, and against which international deck flags fluttered and flapped during Mardi Gras while bilge green anchorage water lapped dully at the barnacles and pilings along the piers.

Hey, you know something? Little Buddy said suddenly after a while, I been thinking about seeing the world like we been talking about and goddammit the thing I don't like about being a sailor is they can't play baseball.

Man, that's the part I don't like either, I said, thinking about how we had always liked wearing pilot caps almost as much as baseball caps. But they can fight and swim.

So that was what I was thinking about when what happened happened this time, but before I could get to what I was going to say about seeing the places on the map and the people I had read about in Geography, we came upon something which stopped everything. I don't remember even blinking but it happened so suddenly that it was as if I had just shut my eyes and opened them and found myself in another place on another day.

The moss shaded trail was making a wide detour away from the edge of the creek to skirt a shallow cypress backwater pond which was clogged with hyacinth pads, and I was on the lookout for water moccasins; but what I suddenly realized I was staring at was a human body.

I saw it first. Then Little Buddy looked and saw it, and we moved in close enough to be absolutely certain about what it was; and it was face down among the green and purple hyacinths. It was floating but it moved only when the breeze made the entanglement of bladder-stemmed hyacinth leaves and backwater debris undulate.

Goddammit, Little Buddy whispered, I knew it.

I don't remember what I said.

I knew it, he said to himself, son-of-a-bitch if I didn't know it.

We were looking from the undergrowth of marsh ferns, reeds and calamus plants and there was the sweet/sour smell of the swamp, with the sunlight filtering through the cypress branches and even the thickest shade was sharp and clear. Little Buddy had drawn the pistol from his mackinaw but all he was doing was holding it in both hands and looking.

There was a musette bag floating off to one side; but I didn't see any fishing or hunting tackle, and you couldn't guess anything from what you could see of what he was wearing because they were just ordinary everyday working clothes. He seemed to be a white man, but you couldn't really be certain about that either. All I could make out was that he was a dead man and he had pale skin and he had been dead long enough to be bloated.

Then I realized that one of the arms was missing and that part of the shoulder had been either torn or eaten away and I couldn't help remembering what I had always heard about gars and crabs ripping strips of flesh from drowned people; and I didn't want to have to see that happening too. But I didn't want to be the one to say let's go and I knew good and well that Little Buddy wasn't going to be the one either. So we both had to stay there, although I wasn't looking at it any more and neither was he, because I looked at him out of the corner of my eye and he wasn't looking at anything.

So I knew I had to figure out something, and I did, and I was watching him and when I saw him trying to steal a look at me, I jerked up as if I had just heard something behind us in the bushes somewhere, and we both started easing back and then I broke and ran, and I knew that he'd be right there running just as hard as I was, and he was.

We ran back the way we had been coming, and the farther we ran the more it seemed that I could still see it, and it seemed that I was smelling it too. The whole swamp seemed to smell like it, and when I had to step in a boggy place it seemed that I was stepping right into the soft dead body itself.

I was running and my neck was hot and my mouth began to taste like green brass, and then I was slowing down, but then it was as if I could see it squelching white, rotten, soggy and slimy like fish meat and I started running again, but I was too tired to run much more and I stopped and Little Buddy sat down on the log and I dropped down beside him.

Hell I ain't going to run no goddamn more, he said, still holding the pistol as if it were a toy.

Me neither, I said.

Goddamn if I run another goddamn step.

We were getting our breath back then, and I was trying to think of what to do next.

Did you hear something? Little Buddy said.

I thought I did, I said lying.

I thought I did, too, he said making us even.

What do you think happened to him?

I don't know. What you think?

I don't know, I said, But the first thing I thought about was bootlegging.

Me too, he said sucking his teeth three times and looking at the pistol as if none of it made any difference to him one way or the other.

Somebody could have shot him and pushed him overboard and he floated in there, I said.

Goddamn right, he said, he could have floated all the way from up in Hog Bayou.

If you already overboard and get shot the cramp will drown you, I said.

Don't care where the bullet hit you, he agreed, putting the pistol back inside his mackinaw and standing up. And I knew he was trying to think about something else because that was what I was also trying to do but I kept wondering how long it would be before somebody else came along as we had done.

Man, he said, suddenly, the goddamn coroner and the goddamn inquest, goddamn!

Man, but any more water lilies drift in there ain't going to be no inquest, I said.

Man, Goddamn, you know it too, he said. Man, God—damn!

So what you want to do now? I said.

You want to let's go on up to Chickasaw?

If you want to.

And cross the trestle going and coming.

If you do.

So we started back up the slope toward where we knew the AT & N was. That was the most direct route to Chickasaw anyway.

We came on back looking for the trail which would take us on out of the cypresses and up the hill and through the hickories and chinquapins to the railroad. We were walking side by side and watching everything then. But as we turned up into the trail, he caught my arm and stopped.

Hey, listen.

I did, and heard footsteps.

Somebody coming!

We scrambled back into a thick clump of bushes and vines and waited, and then we heard them coming nearer, and then we saw them, and there were three of them, and we didn't know any of them. They came on by where we were, one walking in front and the two behind side by side, and two of them were carrying Winchesters.

We were squatting together in our hiding place not even breathing, and they went on down the trail toward the creek.

Peckerwoods, Little Buddy said under his breath. Goddamn peckerwoods.

I bet you they had something to do with it.

I bet so, too. Goddamn peckernose peckerwoods.

You want to let's follow them?

Goddammit, let's follow them goddamn razorback peckerwoods.

I knew he was going to say that, and I wanted to and I didn't want to, but I said all right and we did, and we kept close together in the bushes beside the trail and crept on back down toward the way they had gone.

But when we got to where we could see the creek again, we saw only one of them, and he was standing down by the edge of the water. We waited, watching, and then we saw the other two come paddling up in a rowboat.

They headed the boat into where the one on the bank was waiting and one of them handed him a pair of hip boots and the three of them were talking but we were not close enough to hear what they were saying. Then the one who had been waiting sat on the bank and pulled on the boots and stood and said something else, pointing up the creek, and the boat pulled away, and he was walking along the bank.

We stayed our distance and we could see him and see the two in the boat too, and he was searching along the bank and they were searching along the edge of the water.

I told you so, Little Buddy whispered.

They looking for something all right, I said.

Down in the boat one of them sat on the back end and

paddled and the other one was half standing in the front, using his paddle to move the reeds and lilies.

They sure cain't miss him, I said low to Little Buddy.

Let's watch them do what they going to do.

They went on along the edge of the creek and we were following them, and then we knew that they were getting near where it was, and we stopped and waited. There was a strong breeze blowing from across the creek then but I was sweating and Little Buddy was too.

We saw the one on the bank turn in toward the trees, and we knew exactly where he was, and then we heard him whistle and the boat turned in there and was out of sight too.

They found it, Little Buddy whispered.

Come on.

We better get to a tree.

We scooted to the tree he pointed to and he climbed it and I was right there behind him, and then we were sitting hidden in the moss. You couldn't see them, yet, but we stayed there and waited, and there was no traffic in the channel at all.

I don't know how long we waited, but there was still no traffic, and after a while I saw the boat heading out again, and all three of them were in it. Two of them were rowing then, and the one who had been on the bank was sitting in the back and he was holding the dead man by one foot dragging him in the wake.

Goddamn, Little Buddy said. Look what them goddamn old pecks doing.

Then we realized that the dead man was naked. They had stripped all of his clothes off. They rowed out far enough to see up and down the creek, and then one of the ones rowing stopped and reached out and got what must have been the dead man's boots and knapsack and filled the boots with water and sank them and then tied the knapsack to something and sank that too.

Then they rowed on out into the channel still towing the floating dead man. They headed the boat up toward Chickasaw then, and turned the dead man loose and pulled away as fast as they could go.

We saw them pulling on away and saw the bloated dead man floating on down with the current going on toward the L & N Bridge. They pulled on out of sight, but we still could see the dead body and it looked like a floating sack. I looked back up the way the three men had gone and when I turned and looked at the body again it didn't look like anything but a piece of driftwood, and then it was nothing at all.

We got down out of the tree and started on back along the bank.

I bet you there's a goddamn motherfucking son-of-a-bitching whiskey still up in there somewhere, Little Buddy said. I bet you anything. I bet you a thousand dollars.

Me too, I said. Or maybe a transfer place.

I bet you that's where they gone right now.

Me too.

Goddamn old redneck peckerwood bootleggers.

We were coming on back, and the green and mossy woods were warm and quiet and the only sound was us and the breeze overhead in the trees.

What you want to do now? I said.

Let's cross that goddamn motherfucking son-of-a-bitching shitass trestle.

And if a freight comes, we'll swing down to the crossbeams and let it go over us.

Must have been some time ago.

Must have been.

With him puffed up that big.

I wonder how come they did.

I bet you he must have been spying or stealing or something.

I bet so too.

Do you think they been looking all this time while he was bloating up like that?

I don't know, I said. Maybe when he didn't turn up somewhere so somebody could find him they started looking.

I wonder why they shot him?

I don't know. Maybe because he was a revenue agent.

Maybe so, he said. Maybe he was trying to follow them and they faked him on up into one of the slews and waylaid his ass.

Man if he was a *Yankee* revenue agent them peckerwoods been watching his ass ever since he crossed the Mason-Dixie.

Man that's one thing about a peckerwood, he said. Some of them squint-eyed, nose-talking, bony-butt granny-dodgers don't back up off of nobody when it come to shooting a goddamn rifle and a shotgun.

But Little Buddy was thinking about something else then, because he was frowning to himself without knowing it, and I could tell he was gritting his teeth by the way his temples moved. That was something we both had picked up from Sonny Crenshaw, who said it was something he did instead of chewing tobacco.

But that poor sappin somebody back there, he said suddenly. Suppose he was just out there fishing or something.

Man, I said, but bootleggers can tell when you really fishing or hunting.

Yeah but just suppose, he said. Just suppose he was only

a stranger and it was night and all he was doing was wandering around lost.

We followed the trail on through the Chickasaw thickets and I knitted my brow and shook my head as if I were still trying to figure out something to say about what he had said. But I was thinking about something else then. Because I could still see the bloated corpse among the purple water lilies and the main thing was that someone was dead and gone and his body was nothing but something floating because he was dead and gone dead and gone dead and gone forever.

Then we saw the trestle. It stretched across the ugly bottom like a creosote dragon whose centipede's legs were so many knock-kneed telegraph pole stilts. Little Buddy stopped and took out the pistol. Then he aimed across his forearm and shot three stilts, and the sound went echoing up through Blue Poplar Hollow. Then I took it and shot three more. But there was the also and also of all that from then on even so.

It was as if you had been born hearing and knowing about trains and train whistles, and the same was also true of sawmills and sawmill whistles. I already knew how to mark the parts of the day by sawmill whistles long before I learned to read time as such from the face of a clock.

Sometimes, probably having heard the earliest morning sawmill whistles in my sleep as you sometimes hear neighborhood roosters crowing for daybreak, I used to wake up and lie listening long enough to hear the first-shift hands passing by outside. That was when the daytime fireman relieved the night fireman, and it was also the time when you could hear the logging crews that came that way going to work on that part of Mobile River and Three Mile Creek. These were the putt-boat pilots and the raftmen, some of whom were also skiffboatmen. And there were also the boom men, who used to wear their turned down hip boots (which I also used to call magellan boots and isthmus of panama boots) to and from home, carrying their peavies and hook-and-jam poles angling across their shoulders as pike men did in story books and also as railroad crosstie cutters used to carry their crosscut saws and broadaxes to and from the timber woods.

It was the head day-shift fireman who always blew the next whistle, and that was when the main-shift hands would be coming by. So that was when what you heard passing was not only the log carriage experts like, say, old Sawmill Turner, for instance; but also the shed crews and the yard crews, including the timekeepers and tallymen. But I was usually asleep again by then, and when I woke up for good it would be time to get up and be ready before the first school bell rang.

It would be full daylight then, and by the time you finished breakfast, the first lumber trucks would be grinding their way up out of Sawdust Bottom. And when you heard the next gear shift, that meant they were finally up the hill and leveling off into our flat but somewhat sandy and rutty road to come whining by the gate. Then the next gear-stroke meant that they were ready to pick up speed to fade on away because they had turned onto Buckshaw Road, which was macadamized like Telegraph Road even before the Cochrane Bridge was built and they finally paved it with asphalt like the Chickasaw Highway and made it a part of US 90.

From September through the fall and winter and spring the next thing after the first lumber trucks was always the first school bell. So from then on it was as if you didn't really hear either the sawmills or train whistles (or even boat whistles) anymore until after three o'clock. Because during that part of every day except Saturday and Sunday, everything you did was part of the also and also that school bells and school bell times were all about. Such as singing in 70-degree Fahrenheit schoolroom unison: *Good morning to you good morning to you good morning dear teacher good morning to you.* With your scrubbed hands on the pencil tray desk for roll call and fingernail inspection, with your hair trimmed and combed and brushed and your head erect, your back straight, your shoulders square and your eyes on the exemplary pre-lesson neatness of the janitor-washed blackboard with its semi-permanent border design and theme of the month and motto of the month and chalk colored checkerboard calendar.

Good solo teacher talk among dear children.

Good unison-pupil response-chant morning dear teacher. A very good morning from toothpaste smiles and rainbow ribbons and oilcloth book satchels and brown bag sandwich smells to you Miss So and Miss So and Miss So and So and Miss So-So and Miss So On and Miss So Forth to Miss Metcalf.

Then (when the first kitten mitten mornings of steaming breath and glittering wayside ponds were outside once more) also: *Old Jack Frost is a funny old fellow when the wind begins he begins to bellow. He bites little children on their nose. He bites little children on their toes. He makes little girls say Oh! Oh! Oh! And he makes little boys say Ouch! Ouch! Ouch! He makes little pointed-ats wring hands and blow fingers and say Oh! Oh! Oh! And he makes little nodded-and-smiled-ats shake fists and say Ouch! Ouch!*

Ouch! He makes little sugar and spice and everything nice girls say —! —! —! And he makes little frogs and snails and puppydogtail boys (but not Scooter and not Little Buddy Marshall and not old Cateye Gander Gallagher the Gallinipper) say ——! ——! ——!

But sometimes (especially during afternoon quiet sessions) you could still hear the syrup-green sawdust whine of the log carriage even from that far away, and I could hardly wait to get back home to my own play sawmill, which millwright that I already was I had built complete with boom, rafts, conveyer ramp, carriage, slab and sawdust pile, stacking yard, dry kiln and planer shed, long before the time came to go to school that first year. Because in the summertime in those days I almost always used to become a hard rolling sawmill man as soon as Buckshaw whistle used to blow for high noon no matter what else I was supposed to be at the time. Because that was when you could sit at the sawhorse table outside under the chinaberry tree stripped to the waist like a stacking yard hand, eating new corn and pole beans (or snap beans or string beans) plus new red-skinned potatoes; or butterbeans plus okra; or green (shelled) blackeye peas plus okra; or crowder peas plus okra; along with the very thinnest of all shortening-rich golden crusted corners of cornbread. Not to mention the yellow-flecked mellowness of the home churned buttermilk of those days. Or the homemade lemonade or fresh ice-tea. Especially when you could drink it from your very own quart-size fruit jar not only as if you had been stacking lumber all the morning but also as if all the good cooking in your napkin-covered slat basket had been prepared by your honey brown good-looking wife or woman, who had put on her frilly starched baby doll gingham dress and brought it to where she now sat beside you fanning away the flies in the stacking yard shade.

But all of that was before Miss Lexine Metcalf, and her blue and green and yellow globe revolving on its tilted axis with its North and South Poles, and its Eastern and Western Hemispheres, and its equator plus its Torrid and North Temperate and South Temperate and Frigid Zones and its continents and its oceans and seas and gulfs and great lakes and rivers and basins, and its mountain ranges and plains and deserts and oases, and its islands and peninsulas and archipelagos and capes and horns and straits.

Because from then on (what with her sandtable igloos and wigwams and thatched huts and mud huts and caravan tents and haciendas and chalets and chinese paper houses with lanterns; and what with her bulletin board costumes of many lands and her teacher's desk that could become the Roundtable from which armor-clad knights errant set forth to do battle with dragons and blackboard problems; what with her window box plants that could become Robin Hood's forest and what with her magic pointer that could change everyday Gasoline Point schoolgirls into Cinderellas and Sleeping Beauties and you into Prince Charming or Roland or Siegfried or Sinbad or Ulysses and your Buster Brown shoes or your Keds into Seven League Boots) I was to become a schoolboy above and beyond everything else, for all the absolutely indispensable times I was still to play hooky with Little Buddy Marshall.

What with Miss Lexine Metcalf with whose teacher-pronunciation my given name finally became the classroom equivalent not only of Scooter but also of the other nickname Mama used to call me which was Man which was to say Mama's Man which was to say Mama's Little Man which was to say Mama's Big Man; because Miss Lexine Metcalf was the one who also said it looking at you as if to let you know that she was also calling you what Miss Tee had always called you, which was her mister. *My Mister.*

Hello My Mister. This is My Mister. Show them My Mister.

What with Miss Lexine Metcalf who came to be the one who was there in the classroom. But what also with Miss Tee, from whom had already come ABC blocks and ABC picture books and wax crayon coloring sets, and was the one for whom you learned your first numbers, and who was also the one who said: *This is My Mister who can write his name all by himself. Show them My Mister. This is My Mister who can do addition and subtraction all by himself. Show them My Mister. And show them how My Mister can also recite from the Reader all by himself. The cat said not I. The dog said not I. The little red hen said I will and she did. The little choo choo going up the hill said I think I can I think I can I thought I could I thought I could. Because it tried and it did.*

Sometimes a thin gray, ghost-whispering mid-winter drizzle would begin while you were still at school, and not only would it settle in for the rest of the mist-blurred, bungalow-huddled afternoon, but it would still be falling after dark as if it would continue throughout the night; and even as you realized that such was the easiest of all times to get your homework (even when it was arithmetic) done (no matter what kind of schoolboy you were) you also knew as who hasn't always known that it was also and also the very best of all good times to be where grown folks were talking again, especially when there were the kind of people visiting who always came because there was somebody there from out of town and you could stay up listening beyond your usual time to be in bed.

Their cane bottom chairs and hide bottom chairs and rocking chairs plus stools always formed the same old family-cozy semi-circle before the huge open hearth, and from your place in the chimney corner you could see the play of the firelight against their faces and also watch their tale-time shadows moving against the newspaper wallpaper walls and the ceiling. Not even the best of all barbershops were ever to surpass the best of such nights at home.

They would be talking and rocking and smoking and sometimes drinking, and, aware of the roof sanding, tree-shivering night weather outside, I would be listening, and above us on the scalloped mantlepiece was the old fashioned pendulum clock, which was Papa's heirloom from that ancestral mansion of ante-bellum columns and gingham crisp kitchens in which his mulatto grandmother had herself been an inherited slave until Sherman's March to the Sea but which I still remember as the Mother Goose clock; because it ticked and tocked and ticked and tocked and tocked and struck not only the hours but also the quarter-hours with the soft clanging sound you remember when you remember fairy tale steeples and the rainbow colors of nursery rhyme cobwebs; because it hickory dickory docked and clocked like a brass spoon metronome above the steel blue syncopation of guitar string memories; because it hockey-tock rocked to jangle like such honky tonk piano mallets as echo midnight freight train distances beyond patch-quilt horizons and bedside windowpanes.

Sometimes it would be obvious enough that they were only telling the tallest tales and the most outrageous lies they could either remember or fabricate, and sometimes you could be every bit as certain that their primary purpose was to spell out as precisely as possible the incontestable facts and most reliable figures involved in the circumstance under consideration. But when you listened through the meshes of the Mother Goose clock you already knew long before you came to recognize any necessity to understand (not to mention explain) that no matter which one they said or even believed they were doing they were almost always doing it at least a little of both. (Because even as the Mother Goose clock was measuring the hours and minutes of ordinary days and nights and time tables its tictoculation created that fabulous once upon a time spell under which you also knew that the Jacksonville of the section gang song for instance was really a make-believe place even though you could find it by moving your finger to the right from Pensacola and across Tallahassee on the map of Florida—just as you could find Kansas City by tracing left from St. Louis on the map of Missouri.)

Sometimes there would also be such winter-delicious things as papershell pecans and chinquapins and fresh roasted peanuts to pass around in Mama's pinestraw bowl-basket, and sometimes there was homemade blackberry wine or muscadine wine, and sometimes when it was really a very very special occasion Miss Alzenia Nettleton, who was once a cook in the Governor's Mansion, would either send or bring one of her mouth-melting sweet potato pones. Sometimes when it was blizzard weather there would be a big cast-iron pot of lye hominy (which is something I didn't learn to like until later on), and on some of the best nights the main reason everybody was there in the first place was that it was hog-killing-time weather and somebody had brought Mama the makings of a feast of chitterlings and/or middlings, but of course when that happened the best of the talking seldom if ever got started until the eating was almost over.

Uncle Jerome would always be there unless there was a

fruit boat to be unloaded that night, clearing his throat even when he was not going to say anything, squinting his eyes and making a face and clearing again and swallowing and stretching and rolling his chin because he was a preacher. Because although he had been a longshoreman for the last twenty some odd years and a field hand for some thirty odd years before that, he was supposed to have the Call, although he had never been called by any congregation to be the pastor of any church.

Sometimes Mister Doc Donahue the Dock Hand would also be there. But they wouldn't be drinking just wine with him there. Because leather bellied stevedore that he was he always said that wine was for women and children and Christmas morning fruitcake, and he would get up and get the longshoreman's knapsack he always carried along with his cargo hook and bring out a brown crockery jug of corn whiskey, which always made Papa look over at Mama and get just about tickled to death. They would be passing it around, pouring against the light of the fire, and there would be that aroma then, which I always used to enjoy as much as the smell of warm cigar ashes and freshly opened Prince Albert tobacco cans.

They would talk on and on, and then (when somebody mentioned something about the weather itself and somebody else said Yeah but talking about some weather,) you could always tell you were going to hear about the great Juvember Storm again, and sometimes that would be what they spent the rest of the night telling about, each one telling it as he remembered it from where he was at the time, with Uncle Jerome telling his as if it all had been something happening in the Bible, although nobody, not even he, ever claimed that it had actually stormed for forty days and forty nights. But Uncle Jerome always pointed out that everything under the sun was in the Bible including automobiles, because old Ezekiel saw the wheel in the middle of the wheel, and what was an airship but a horseless chariot in the sky, and if somebody didn't cut in on him he would stand up and begin walking the floor and preaching another one of his sermons.

Everybody had his own way of telling about it, but no matter how many parts were added you always saw the main part the same way: rivers and creeks rising and over-flowing the back country, washing houses off their foundations and sometimes completely away; bales of cotton and barrels of flour and molasses and cans of lard floating out of warehouses and scattering through the swamps; horses neighing and cows lowing and trying to swim but drowning because (so they used to say) their behinds sucked in so much water; people living in barns and hay lofts and pad-dling everywhere in skiff boats, people camping in lean-to tent cities in the hills like hobos. People camping on the bluffs like Indians, people camping on timber rafts like the early settlers; trains not running because not only were the tracks washed out but in some places whole spans of bridges had been swept loose. . . .

Then afterwards, there was the epidemic during which even more perished than during the storm itself. But all of that was always a part of the storm story also. And that was when Uncle Jerome always used to say God was warn-ing sinners that He could do it again although He had promised that it would be the fire next time, and he would get up and start clearing his throat and making faces and walking the floor again and then he would go on to show you how even in the almighty act of bringing the flood again God had also brought the fire next time after all. Be-cause what so many many people had suffered and died from was the FEVER, which meant that they were being consumed in a fire more terrible than brimstone! Mess around with mortal man born in sin and shaped in inequity but Gentlemen Sir don't you never start trying to mess with God.

But Papa, whose given name was Whit probably for Whitley but maybe for Whitney and so was sometimes called Papa Whit and sometimes Unka Whit, who had not been inside a church except to attend somebody's funeral since he was baptized thirty some odd years ago, would then take another swallow from his whiskey glass and wipe his mouth and wink at Mister Doc the Dock Hand and look over at Mama because he knew good and well she was going to be scandalized to mortification and say Amen God sure did work a mysterious way His wonders or His blessings or whichever it was to bestow because that was the same storm that had made more good paying jobs for our folks in that country than anything else till the war came.

What I always used to call Papa was Papoo and he used to call me his little gingerbrown papoose boy, which may have been why I called him Papoo in the first place. He himself was as white as any out and out white man I have ever seen in my life. And no wonder either, because not only was he said to be a whole lot more than just half white, it was also said quite accurately that he was acknowledged by most of his white blood relatives much more readily than he himself was ever willing to acknowledge any of them (except when it came to such legal matters as clearing titles to property inherited in common). I myself once overheard Mama telling Aunt Callie the Cat Callahan that the main reason we had moved down into Mobile County when the war boom came was to get away from Papa's white kinfolks in the country. And another time I heard her telling Miss Sadie Womack about how red Papa's ears used to turn when the white people back in the country used to see him driving her into town in the buckboard and pretend that they thought she was not his wife but only one of his black field hands.

Papa himself never talked about white people as such. But sometimes when they were talking about hard times, somebody would get him to tell about some of the things he had seen and done during those times when he had to go off somewhere and pass for white to get a job. That was something to hear about also, and one time when I was telling Little Buddy Marshall about it the next day, he said: Everybody say, don't care how much of his skin and his keen nose and his flat ass Mister Whit might have got from the whitefolks, he got his mother-wit from the getting place. That's how come you don't never catch nobody calling him no old shit-colored peckerwood behind his back.

There was also that time with that white man downtown by the marine store on Government Street. He and Papa knew each other and they were laughing and talking and I was having a good time looking in store windows, and I went looking all the way up to the sporting goods store, and when I came back they were talking about a job; and the man said something about something both of them had been doing somewhere, and that brought up something else, and I heard the man say Papa was a fool for being a durned ole niggie when he could be a wyat man. Hell Whit you as wyat as I am any durned day of the week be durned if you ain't, and Papa just shook his head and said You don't understand, Pete.

Midwinter nights around the fireplace was one of the times when Soldier Boy Crawford used to tell about crossing the Atlantic Ocean and about the mines and the torpedoes and the submarines, and then about the French places he had been to, and sometimes he would mix in a lot of French words with what he was saying such as bon-

jour come on tally voo and such as sand meal killing my
trees easy to Paree and such as donay me unbootay cornyak
silver plate and such as voo lay voo zig zig and so on, screw-
ing up his face and narrowing his shoulders as well as his
eyes and wiggling his fingers as if he were playing the words
as notes on a musical instrument.

When you heard him talking about France in the barbershop he was usually telling either about the Argonne
Forest or the Hindenburg Line or about French women
whom he called frog women. But what he used to talk
mostly about at the fireside was the kind of farming country they had over there, especially the wine making country.
And he would also tell about the mountain country and the
churches which he said had the finest bells and the keenest
steeples and the prettiest windows in the world: Talking
about some stain glass church windows y'all ain't seen no
stain glass church windows y'all ain't seen no church statues
and I ain't talking about no wood I'm talking about natural
stone nine hundred years old.

What he used to tell about Paris at such times was
mostly about the buildings and the streets with the cafes on
the sidewalk and the parks and the cabarets, and that was
also when he used to tell about eating horse meat, snails
and frogs legs (but not about the pissoirs and the bidets
and best of all the poules from whom came french kissing).
He would always say Gay Paree was the best city in the
world, and that was also when he would always say A man
is a man over there and if somebody said as somebody as
often as not did that a man ain't nothing but a man nowhere, you knew he was going to say Yeah but that ain't
what *I'm* talking about, what I'm talking about is somewhere you can go anywhere you big enough to go and do
anything you big enough to do and have yourself some of

anything you got the money to pay for. That's what I'm talking about.

Soldier Boy Crawford, (who during blizzard weather also used to wear his woolen wraparound leggings along with his Army coat and overseas cap and who also had a steel helmet that looked like a wash basin but which he called his doughboy hat and who was said to have brought back a German Luger plus some hand grenades plus a bayonet, a musette bag and a gas mask too because he for one was never going to let them catch him with his pants down if he could help it) was the main one who used to tell me and Little Buddy Marshall about all of the things Luzana Cholly had done during the war. Because old Luze himself never did talk about any of that, not even when you asked him about it. Sometimes he used to say he was going to save it and tell us about it when we were old enough to understand it, and sometimes he would answer one or two questions about something, say, like how far Big Bertha could shoot, and how the Chau-Chau automatic rifle worked and things like that. But you could never get him to sit down and tell about the actual fighting like Soldier Boy Crawford did. Once you got Soldier Boy Crawford worked up he was subject to fight the whole war all over again.

The rain that was falling then would be crackling down on the shingles of the gabled roof of that house, and the fire in the hearth would sparkle as Papa poked it, and he would be in his same chair in his same place in the corner; and sometimes they would be telling about some of the same old notorious rounders and roustabouts that the guitar players and the piano players made up songs about. Especially if Mister Doc Donahue was there, because he was the one who could always remember something else about old

63

John Henry, who went with blue steel sparks, and old John Hardy, who went with greased lightning. Once he held the floor all night just describing how old Stagolee shot and killed Billy Lyons, and what happened at that famous trial.

Mister Doc Donahue was also the one who used to tell about how old Robert Charles declared war on the city of New Orleans and fought the whole police force all by himself with his own special homemade bullets. But the best of all the old so-called outlaws he used to tell about was always the one from Alabama named Railroad Bill. Who was so mean when somebody crossed him and so tricky that most people believed that there was something supernatural about him. He was the one that no jail could hold overnight and no bloodhounds could track beyond a certain point. Because he worked a mojo on them that nobody ever heard of before or since. And the last time he broke jail, they had the best bloodhounds in the whole state there to track him. But the next morning they found them all tied together in a fence corner near the edge of the swamp, not even barking anymore, just whining, and when they got them untangled they were ruined forever, couldn't scent a polecat and wouldn't even run a rabbit; and nobody ever saw or came near hide nor hair of old Railroad Bill from that time on.

Naturally the whitefolks claimed they caught him and lynched him; but everybody knew better. The whitefolks were always claiming something like that. They claimed that they had caught old Pancho Villa and hung him for what he had done out in New Mexico; and they claimed that they had hemmed up old Robert Charles in a steeple and burned him alive; and they also claimed that Jessie Willard had salivated old Jack Johnson down in Havana that time! Well, they could go around bragging about how the great white hope had put the big black menace back in his place and proved white supremacy all they wanted to, but everybody knew that Jack Johnson who was married to a white woman had to trade his world championship in for his American citizenship, and thirty thousand dollars to get back in the USA and there was a picture in every barbershop which showed him letting himself be counted out, lying shading his eyes from the Cuban sun, lying with his legs propped like somebody lying on the front porch; and as for Jessie Willard, everybody knew he couldn't even stand up to Jack Dempsey, who was the same Jack Dempsey who brought back old John L. Sullivan's color line because he didn't ever intend to get caught in the same ring with the likes of Jack Johnson, Sam Langford or even somebody like Harry Wills, not even with a submachine gun. Everybody knew that.

The whitefolks claimed that they had finally caught up with old Railroad Bill at some crossroads store somewhere and had slipped up on him while he was sitting in the middle of the floor sopping molasses with his gun lying off to one side, and they swore that they had blown the back of his head off with a double barrel charge of triple-ought buckshot. But in the first place Railroad Bill didn't eat molasses, and in the second place he didn't have to break into any store to get something to eat. Because folks kept him in plenty of rations everywhere he went by putting out buckets of it in certain special places for him mostly along the Railroad which was what his name was all about; and in the third place he must have broken into more than fifty stores by that time and he just plain didn't rob a store in the broad open daylight, not and then sit down in the middle of the floor and eat right there; and in the fourth place there was at least a dozen other mobs in at least a dozen other places all claiming that they had been the ones who laid him low, each one of them telling a completely different tale about how and when and where it all happened. Some claimed that they had hung him upside down on the drawbridge and then riddled him and left what was left of him there for the buzzards. But they never settled on which bridge.

I didn't know very much about history then. Which was what all that about Uncle Walt and the bloodhounds was all about too. Because I knew even while it was happening that it wasn't just happening then. I didn't know very much about historical cause and effect then, but I knew enough to realize that when something happened it was a part of something that had been going on before, and I wasn't surprised at all that time when I was awakened in the middle of the night and got up and saw Uncle Walt sitting by the fire in Papa's clothes talking about how he had made his way through Tombigbee Swamp. He slept in Uncle Jerome's bed and Uncle Jerome slept on a pallet in front of the fireplace. They put ointment on the bruises and rubbed his joints down in Sloan's Liniment, and he slept all day the next day and all the day after that too, telling about it again the second night by the fire with his feet soaking in a tub of hot salt water, and I could see it all and I was in it too, and it was me running through the swamps, hearing them barking, coming, and it was me who swam across the creek and was running wet and freezing in the soggy shoes all the next day. Hungry and cold but not stopping even when I didn't hear them anymore, and not hopping a freight either, because they would be looking for you to do that. It was me who made my way because I knew that country like the Indians knew it, and I knew the swamps and the streams like the old keelboat men and I knew the towns and villages like a post rider, and then it was me who was long gone like a Natchez Trace bandit.

I saw Uncle Walt sitting there in the firelight not afraid but careful, talking about how he was going to make it across the Mason-Dixon, and I didn't really know anything at all about whatever it was he had done or hadn't done, and I still don't know what it was, but I knew that whatever it was it was trouble, and I said It's like once upon a time back then. Because that's what Mama always said, who knew it from her grandfather, who was Uncle Walt's grandfather too, who knew it from his father when there was no hope of foot rest this side of Canada, which was also called Canaan, which was the Promised Land, and I also knew that all of that was about something called the Underground Railroad, which ran from the House of Bondage to the land of Jubilo.

They were always talking about freedom and citizenship, and that was something else that Uncle Jerome used to start preaching about. He had all kinds of sermons ready for times like that. Sometimes he would be talking about children of Israel, and sometimes it would be the walls of Jericho, and sometimes it would be the big handwriting on the wall which was also the BIG HAND writing on the wall which was also the Big Hand writing on the WAR. That was when he used to say that the color of freedom was blue. The Union Army came dressed in blue. The big hand that signed the freedom papers signed them in blue ink which was also blood. The very sky itself was blue, limitless (*and gentlemen, sir, before I'd be a slave, I'll be buried in my grave*). *And I said My name is Jack the Rabbit and my home is in the briarpatch.*

Sometimes he would also say that the freedom road was a road through the wilderness and sometimes it wasn't any road at all because there never was any royal road to freedom for anybody (so don't you let nobody turn you round. And don't you let nobody know too much about your business either. And I said Call me Jack the Bear on my way somewhere).

Then it would be Education again. They didn't ever get tired of talking about that, the old folks telling about how they learned to spell and write back in the old days when they used to use slate tablets and the old Blueback Webster. The old days when they used to have to hold school whenever and wherever they could. Whenever they could spare the time from working the crops and wherever the teacher could find a place to shelter them. Whenever there was a teacher.

Then later on I was the one they meant when they said the young generation was the hope and glory. Because I had come that far in school by then; and sometimes it was Geography and sometimes it was History, and sometimes I had to tell about it, and sometimes I had to get the book and read it to them. Especially when it was about the Revolutionary War. Sometimes I had to read about Columbus too, and sometimes it would also be the explorers and the early settlers. But most of the time what they wanted to hear about was how the original thirteen colonies became the first thirteen states and who said what and who did what during that time and how the Constitution was made and who the first Presidents were and what they did.

That was also when I used to love to recite the Declaration of Independence, and the Gettysburg Address for them; and I could also recite the Preamble to the Constitution and part of the Emancipation Proclamation; and I could also quote from the famous speeches of Patrick Henry and James Otis and Citizen Tom Paine; and I knew all kinds of sayings from *Poor Richard's Almanac.*

That boy can just about preach that thing right now, Mister Jeff Jefferson said one night after I had recited the

68

William Lloyd Garrison and Frederick Douglass parts from the National Negro History Week pageant.

That boy can talk straight out of the dictionary when he want to, Mister Big Martin said looking at me but talking to everybody.

It just do you good to hear that kind of talk.

Whitefolks need to hear some talk like that.

The whitefolks the very one said all that, Jeff.

What kind of whitefolks talking like that?

Histry-book whitefolks.

What kind of histry-book whitefolks?

Whitefolks in that same book that child reading.

I ain't never heard no whitefolks believing nothing like that in all of my born days.

Whitefolks printed that book, didn't they?

I don't care who printed that book, that's *freedom* talk.

Well, the histry book whitefolks got up the Constitution, didn't they?

Yeah, and there was some histry book blackfolks in there somewhere too, you can just about bet on that. There was a jet-black roustabout right in there with old Christopher Columbus, and the very first one to try to climb that bunker hill was a mean black son-of-a-gun from Boston. Ain't nothing never happened and wasn't some kind of a black hand mixed up in it somewhere. You just look at it close enough. The very first ones to come up with iron was them royal black Ethiopians.

You right about that, Mister Big Martin said, ain't nobody going to dispute you about that.

I know I'm right, Mister Jeff said, And I still say these whitefolks need to hear some of that kind of gospel. These ain't no histry book whitefolks around here and this ain't no histry. This ain't nothing but just a plain old everyday mess!

Trying to keep the black man down.

All whitefolks ain't like that, Phil.

Yeah, but them that is.

And some of us too, Jesus, Miss Minnie Ridley Stovall said, Lord the truth is the light, and some of us just ain't ready yet.

Amen, Mister Big Martin said.

Amen? Mister Phil Motley said. What you mean Amen?

That's what I want to know, Mister Jeff Jefferson said.

I mean the truth is the light just like Minnie say.

I done told you, Miss Minnie Ridley Stovall said.

Well ain't none of these peckerwoods around here ready for nothing neither, but just look at them. That's some truth for the light too.

Yeah but I still say some of us still ain't learned how to stick together yet.

Now Big'un, you know good and well that can get to be a horse of another color, Mister Doc Donahue said. I for one don't never intend to be sticking with any and everybody coming along because he say he one of us. You know better than that.

That's why I say some of us, Jesus, Miss Minnie Ridley Stovall said.

That's all right about all that, Mister Big Martin said. I'm talking about when you talking about going up against that stone wall. I want us to be ready. I'm talking about Stonewall Jackson. I'm talking about Jericho. That's what I'm talking about.

Well, we talking about the same thing then, Mister Phil Motley said.

That's all right about your Stonewall Jackson too, Mister Jeff Jefferson said, and your Vardaman and your Pitchfork

Ben and all the rest of them. This child right here is getting old Stonewall Jackson's water ready.

They were all laughing then. Because everybody in Gasoline Point knew how Shorty Hollingsworth had met his waterloo and got the name Hot Water Shorty. His wife had come up behind him and dashed a pot of scalding lye water down the seat of his pants while he was sitting on the front steps cleaning his shotgun and bragging about what he was going to do if she didn't have his supper on the table in the next five minutes. He had yelled, dropped his shotgun and lit out across the barbwire fence and hadn't stopped until he was chin deep in Three Mile Creek. He had a new name from then on and he also had a new reputation: he could outrun a striped-assed ape.

Uncle Jerome said I was learning about verbs and adverbs and proverbs; and he preached his sermon on the dictionary that time, and he had his own special introduction to the principles of grammar: A noun is someone or something; a pronoun is anything or anybody; a verb is tells and does and is; an adverb is anyhow, anywhere, anytime; an adjective is number and nature; a preposition is relationship; and conjunction is membership; and interjection is the spirit of energy.

Then that time when Aunt Sue was visiting us from Atmore, old Mayfield Turner was there. Old Sawmill Turner, the log carriage expert, who Mama said had been trying to marry Aunt Sue for more than seventeen years, which meant that he had started before she married her first husband (she was visiting us because she had just separated from her fourth husband). Old Sawmill was wearing his blue pinstripe, tailor-made suit and his Edwin Clapp shoes and smelling like the barbershop and sitting cross-legged like Henry Ford; and every time he took a puff on his

White Owl, he flashed his diamond ring like E. Berry Wall. Sometimes when they were talking about him behind his back they used to give him names like John D. Rockefeller Turner and J. P. Morgan Turner and Jay Gould Turner because he also sported pearl gray kidskin gloves, and he was always talking about stocks and bonds and worrying about the National Debt.

I was reading about Valley Forge that night, and I knew he was there just as I knew that Mister Lige and Miss Emma Tolliver and Bro Mark Simpkins and his wife, Miss Willeen were all there, because they were always the first ones to come by to see Aunt Sue when she was in town. But at first the only ones that I was really conscious of were Miss Lula Crayton and Miss Liza Jefferson, because every time I paused Miss Lula Crayton kept saying Tribulation tribulation trials and tribulation, and Miss Ida Jefferson would respond one time as if she were hearing some new gossip, and the next time as if I were reading the Bible itself (saying Honey don't tell me, saying Lord have mercy Jesus).

Then I happened to glance up and see old Sawmill again, and he had stopped puffing on his cigar. He was leaning forward with his hand under his chin, his eyes closed, his lips moving, repeating everything I was reading, word for word. He had forgotten all about Aunt Sue, for the time being at least. I was reading about how the Redcoats were wining and dining and dancing warm in Philadelphia while the ragtag bobtail Continental Army was starving and freezing in makeshift huts and hovels, and about how General George Washington himself had to get out and personally whip slackers and stragglers and would-be deserters back into the ranks with the flat of his sword. All of which was what Give me liberty or give me death really meant, which was why whenever you talked about following in the footsteps of our great American forefathers you were also talking about the bloody tracks the half barefooted troops left in the snow that fateful winter.

Everytime I glanced up I could see old Sawmill Turner still leaning forward toward me, his lips still moving, the tip of his cigar gone to ash. Then when I came to the end of the chapter and closed the book, he stood up and stepped out; into the center of the semi-circle as Uncle Jerome always did. I'm a histry scholar myself, he said. I been a histry scholar ever since I first saw all of them seals and emblems down at the post office when I was a little boy back in Lowdnes County. Then he ran his hand down into his pocket and pulled out a fat roll of brand-new greenbacks, which he held against his chest like a deck of gambling cards. He peeled off a crisp one-dollar bill and held it up and said, Old George Washington is number one because he was first in war and first in peace and first in the hearts of his countrymen. He got it started.

And old Abe Lincoln. (*He held up a five-dollar bill.*) Came along later on and had to save the Union. Old Alexander Hamilton didn't get to be the President, but he was in there amongst them when they started talking about how they were going to handle the money, and here he is. (*He pulled off a ten-dollar bill.*) And here's old Tom Jefferson. (*Off came a twenty-dollar bill.*) Now he was a educated man and he knowed exactly what to do with his book learning. And then you come on up to old Ulysses S. Grant. (He held up a fifty-dollar bill without even pausing.) He was the one old Abe Lincoln himself had to send for when the going got tight, and later on they made him the eighteenth President.

He held up the fifty-dollar bill long enough for everybody to see that it really was a fifty-dollar bill and then he held up a hundred-dollar bill and said, Old Ben Franklin didn't ever even want to be the President. But old Ben Franklin left just as big a mark in histry as any of them. They didn't put him up there on no one-hundred-dollar bill for nothing. Old Ben Franklin was one of the smartest men they had back in them days, and everybody give him his due respect. Old Ben Franklin told them a lot of good points about how to put them clauses in the Constitution. He was just about the first one they thought about when they had to send somebody across the water to do some official business for the Government with them fast talking Frenchmen. And talking about being cunning, old Ben Franklin was the one that took a kite and a Cocola bottle and stole naked lightning.

He came and stood in front of my chair then. This boy is worth more than one hundred shares of gilt-edged preferred, and the good part about it is we all going to be drawing down interest on him. Then he handed me a five-dollar bill as crisp as the one he had held up before, and told me to buy myself a fountain pen; and he told Mama he was going to be the one to stake me to all the ink and paper I needed as long as I stayed in school. All I had to do was show him my report card.

All I could do was say thank you, and I said I would always do my best. And Miss Lula Crayton said Amen. And Miss Liza Jefferson said God bless the lamb and God bless you Mayfield Turner. Then before anybody else could say anything he excused himself and Aunt Sue walked him to the door and he put on his alpaca topcoat, his black Homburg hat and his Wall Street gloves and was gone.

All Mama could do was wipe her eyes, and all Papa could do was look at the floor and shake his head and smile. But Uncle Jerome was on his feet again, saying he was talking about the word made manifest for Manifest Destiny; and I knew he was going to take over where Sawmill Turner

74

had left off and preach a whole sermon with me in it that night. And so did everybody else, and they were looking at me as if I really had become the Lamb or something. So I looked at the mantlepiece, and I heard the Mother Goose clock and outside there was the Valley Forge bitter wind in the turret-tall chinaberry tree.

When you looked out from the chinaberry tree south-east across the L & N clearing and that part of Mobile River and Polecat Bay you were also looking toward the Tensaw canebrakes beyond which was the horizon blue territory of the Old Spanish Fort, about which there were fireside and swingporch tales that were also about the Old Spanish Trail.

There was a time when I used to think it was called the Old Spanish Trail because of all the low hanging Spanish moss such as you saw from the picnic truck on the way to such shrimp and oyster and crab gumbo and baseball towns as Bayou La Batre and Pascagoula and Biloxi. So when they used to sit talking about the olden days when the explorers and pirates used to come ashore it was as if the Old Spanish

Main had been so named because you had to bushwack
your way through all that Spanish moss to get to the coast
and see the Jolly Roger seadog schooner sails bounding
suddenly into view from the foggy nina-pinta-santamaria
gray Spanish distance beyond the horizon.

Once there had also been an Old French Fort. But that
was now known as Twenty-Seven Mile Bluff. I had never
been there, but I knew that it was supposed to be that many
more miles farther up Mobile River so I also knew that it
was something else you were sighting in the direction of
when you swung your spyglass around to the northeast and
saw the sky falling away beyond Chickasabogue Swamp and
Hog Bayou. It was not until later on in Miss Gale's Alabama
History class that I was to find out that Twenty-Seven Mile
Bluff was supposed to have been the site where the
original French colonists had settled Mobile itself. That was
when we were learning about how Mobile came to be
known as the City of Five Flags, and that was also when I
found out that the original name had been Fort St. Louis
de la Mobile, because Mobile was the name of the Indians
living on Twenty-Seven Mile Bluff before the first Frenchmen arrived with such weather-beaten cannons and wrought
iron fountains and benches and gallery grillwork as you still
saw in and around Bienville Square and up and down Dau-
phine and Royal and Conti, not to mention Government
Street.

But I already knew something about the five flags before that because I had been seeing all of them fluttering
and snapping above the downtown sidewalk decorations
along the Mardi Gras parade route every year long before
I was yet old enough to start to school. So I am almost
certain that I had already heard Soldier Boy Crawford explaining which one was French and which was Spanish and
which English long before I had ever heard of Miss Lexine

Metcalf, to say nothing of Miss Gale. Because I can remember him coming to the soldier's position of attention and saluting as he named each one, but when he came to the Confederate flag he would always thumb his nose and slap his backside and call it the shit rag of the goddamn slavery time peckerwoods who fought against the Union because they wanted to keep the black man bound down in servitude under the white man.

If you could have seen the L & N flagstop from the china-berry tree you could also have seen the Chickasabogue Bridge and the shallows where the gulls circled and dipped and swooped above what was left of the old *Clotilde*, which some people used to call the old Flotilla, and others the old Crowtillie, but which I later came to realize had been the very same ship Unka JoJo the African had always been talking about when somebody asked him to tell once more about coming across the big water back in 'fifty-nine, which, I was to learn still later on, was one of the last if not the very last shipload of African captives (one hundred and sixteen) to be bootlegged directly into the continental limits of the United States before the outbreak of the War for Emancipation.

At first what I used to think Unka JoJo was talking about was the Journey of Jonah in the Belly of the Whale (what with him actually insisting over and over that that was how he came to be in Nineveh, even as so many others in church and out were forever declaring that we were all the Children of Israel on our way out of our sojourn of bondage in Egyptland). Because as far as I was ever concerned at first, Unka JoJo the African was nothing, if not the most venerable local embodiment of all biblical prophets, apostles and disciples anyway. He wore the Afro-Chinese thin chin whiskers of a seer and sayer and wiseman, and I had no doubt whatsoever that his twisted ashy brown walking stick could become a snake, a burning bush, a divining rod, a lightning rod, or anything else he willed it to be anytime he threw it down and snapped his fingers and uttered the magic African biblical words.

Then there was also the even more obvious fact that as sexton of African Hill Baptist Church he was not only the one pulling the rope when you heard the African Hill Baptist bell tolling (as softly as if black crepe mourning veils were being hung out across the sky on a clothesline attached to a kite), he was also the one who kept the keys to the big French lace wrought iron gate to African Baptist Hill Graveyard and so was also the one who knew exactly which six-foot plot of earth would be allotted to the next person to die. (Which was why when Little Buddy Marshall and I used to mimic Unka JoJo's stick tapping, dicty-rocking, one-step-drag-foot, catch-up shuffle walk we knew very well indeed that we were flirting with bad luck, because doing that you were not only getting pretty close to imitating and thereby mocking the inevitable infirmities of old age which you were supposed to have been born knowing better than to do, but you were also just one step away from thumbing your nose while somebody was praying or saying the Blessing, which was the next worse thing to cutting a caper while the preacher was saying ashes to ashes and dust to dust, something that only the babylonian people in the voodoo town of New Orleans were said to dare to do.

As for Unka JoJo being an African, at first I used to think Africa was short for African Hill Neighborhood. So I used to say: Okay, so they might have red clay hills and the Southern Railroad and African Baptist, but in Gasoline Point we have two creeks plus the river plus the L & N; and they can have their fig trees and scuppernong arbors and plum thickets and yard peas and gourd vines, and they can make all the elderberry wine they want to, because we have all the best blackberry slopes this side of Chickasaw plus almost all of the trees with the best muscadine vines, so we make that kind of wine; and we also live closer to the swamps and bayous and the whiskey stills, which is why we have the best jook houses and the greatest jookhouse piano players in the world.

And when somebody from up there used to call us them old sawmill quarters niggers, section gang niggers and foggy bottom niggers who didn't come from anywhere but from looking up a mule's ass back on the old plantations back in slavery times, all I thought was that they were trying to get even because we were also not only closer to all the best places for hunting both land game and water game, but we also had a baseball team that was in the same class as those from Chickasaw and Whistler and Maysville and Bayou La Batre and Biloxi.

It was not until I finally began to pay close enough attention during the New Year's Day ceremonies celebrating the Emancipation Proclamation that I began to become aware of the everyday flesh and blood geographical facts and historical circumstances that the old *Clotilde* had once been a part and parcel of. But from then on you could also understand that there was indeed a fundamental similarity as well as an all-important difference between the Belly of the Whale and the Bowels of Middle Passage. Because back when I still used to think the Emancipation Commemoration Day speakers were saying not Abraham Lincoln but able hammer link gone and used to visualize the brawniest of plantation blacksmiths (with Arm & Hammer soda box muscles) cutting links of chain gang shackles with a cold chisel and a pig iron anvil, I also used to think the old *Clotilde* had once been a United Fruit Company boat on which Unka JoJo had come across the Gulf from somewhere in the Caribbean as had Blue Gum Silas the pigeon-toed West Indian (who was also known as Geechee Silas and as the Blue Gum Geechee because of the abba abba way he talked and because he was so crazy about rice like the abba abba talking Portugese or Portageechee sailors).

Anyway it was some time before I was to think any more about Unka JoJo being an African than about Blue Gum Geechee Silas the West Indian handyman or about Jake Hugh or JQ or Jacques Martinet the Creole fish and oyster peddler or about Chastang Cholly the Cajun nightwatchman or Chief Big Duck the Chickasaw Indian or Lil Duck the Choctaw Indian or Miss Queen Minnie Jo-Buck who was supposed to be a Black Creek Indian because she had coal black velvet-smooth skin and jet black glossy hair that came all the way down to her waist. Because as many times as I had tapped my imaginary walking stick and made my voice tremble mimicking the abba abba geechee talk of Unka JoJo saying All the time free in the old country, I still didn't realize that he was talking about coming all the way across the Atlantic Ocean from another continent and another hemisphere until I learned to use the globe for Miss Lexine Metcalf.

Then that day in the barbershop Papa Gumbo Willie McWorthy looked out and saw him coming hitch stepping along Buckshaw Road and said: Goddamn, deliver me from all that old dried-up-assed elephant hocky about how he used to be so goddamn free and equal back over somewhere in Africa. Like he supposed to be better than somebody because them old Rebs fired on Fort Sumter before the man had a chance to sell his ass off up the river to pick cotton on the plantation like our old folks used to have to do. Deliver me from all that old abba abba bullshit about them Hill niggers being some kind of pure-blooded Africans. Because if that ain't trying to play the dozens on everybody down here I sure would like to know what is.

He also said: Yeah, my daddy come from off of old Marster's old plantation, and my mammy used to belong to some white folks by the name of Shelby. Hell, wasn't but just six years between me myself and slavery times. My daddy used to say as far as he could figure and recollect he must have been born somewhere around eighteen and forty-one, and my mammy told me they told her they had papers to say she was born in 'forty-six. And I was born in 'seventy-one, six years after Surrender.

That was also the day when Soldier Boy Crawford said: You know what I tell them? This what I always tell them. I tell them don't make no goddamn difference to me. And I mean it. What the goddamn hell I care? You know what I tell them? The same thing I told them goddamn Germans. Fuck that shit. Let's go. Them som'iches over there talking about Nigger where your tail at. I said up your mama's ass, motherfucker, and this goddamn cold steel bayonet right here up yours. Because that's what I say. Don't make a goddamn bit of difference to me if my goddamn granddaddy was a goddamn tadpole, LET'S GO. Because I'm the som'ich right here ready to go up side your head. Don't care if my poor old grandmammy wasn't nothing but a stump hole, LET'S GO. And that's exactly the same thing I say when another one of them Hill Africans come trying to make out like his granddaddy used to be sitting on a solid gold diamond studded stool somewhere on the left-handed side of the Zulu River with his own niggers waiting on him. I say that's all right with me. LET'S GO. I say, Man, my old granddaddy was so dumb Old Marster wouldn't even trust him to pick cotton. I say Old Marster used to say the only thing my poor old granddaddy was good for was mixing cowshit and horseshit on the compost pile, so maybe that's how come I'm so full of bullshit. BUT THAT'S ALL RIGHT WITH ME, LET'S GO.

But sometimes he also used to like to tell about some of the Africans he had seen in France during the war. That was when he used to talk about how the Senegalese were never supposed to unsheath their swords and daggers and even their bayonets without drawing some human blood with them before putting them back, so when they got faked into pulling them at the wrong time they always had to cut themselves. To keep from breaking the rule about always meaning business and never woofing when it comes to weapons. And that was when he also used to say that the Germans said they would stop using gas warfare if France and Uncle Sam would promise to pull the niggers and Africans out of the front lines and put them all in the Quartermaster's and the Engineer's work battalions.

Now talking about somebody black, he said, Old Unka JoJo supposed to be pure blood African, but that just go to show you because he ain't all that black at all. Hell, he more rusty brown than even chocolate colored. But, gentlemens, them goddamn Sneegeleese sure enough black. And I'm talking about when you so black you blue-black. But you want to know something the blackest som'iches I ever seen in my life wasn't even no Africans at all. I seen some goddamn Hindu Indians blacker than everybody up there on African Hill. Gentlemens, I seen some goddamn Hindu Indians in Paris, France blacker than hair!

❀

Mama was not talking about us and the Africans that day when she said what she said about not playing the dozens. She was talking about Bubber Joe Davis and String-bean Patterson, who had just been arrested and taken to jail because they had started out making jokes and signifying about each other's kinfolks and then had ended up shooting at each other. But, as was almost always the case, what she said was also something I was supposed to apply to myself when the time came (as it did soon enough): Don't make a bit of difference in the world where you come from you still got to do the best you can with what you come here with. Don't care if it ain't nothing else but just your health and strength, you better be thankful for that instead of going around trying to make out like you born with some kind of silver spoon in your mouth. Lord, I get so sick and tired of folks got to always be up somewhere putting on some kind of old airs for somebody to think they so much. Anytime any of them come up playing you in some kind of old dozens you just stay out of it. You just tell them I say the Christchild was born in a stall.

And laid in a manger, Uncle Jerome said coming in from the back room, and wrapped in swattling clothes. Don't take my word for it. Read the Bible. The Son of God was thuswise born and the son of man just better be glad to get here any way he can, considering he ain't nothing but clay except for the spirit, and considering except for the soul six foot of clay is exactly where he going to end up. Vanity of vanity all is vanity. That's what the Bible tells us. And it also say man born of a woman is but a few days and they are fraught full of trouble. So you tell them I say they ain't got no time to be playing no dozens. You tell them I say they better leave them dozens to God. Tell them I say God the one had TWELVE disciples and put TWELVE months in the year and marked TWELVE hours on the face of the clock. And why in the name of God do you think we count eggs by the dozens and not the five, ten, fifteen, twenties? Because the egg is the genesis and the revelation of life. Tell them I say if they just got to play some dozens go hunt some Easter Eggs. No, but they don't want nothing to do with something like that, because that's the CLEAN dozens and what they always subject to have on their dirty minds is the DIRTY dozens.

I don't remember that Miss Tee, who was the one who always came next after Mama and was already there long before Miss Lexine Metcalf, ever mentioned anything at all to me about the dozens as such. But then it was as if the only twelve that ever had any special significance for her in those days was the one that came after the Eleventh Grade. In any case so far as she was ever concerned there was no family name or ancestral bloodlines of identity and inheritance that was likely to stand you in much better stead than the also and also of the background you could create for yourself by always doing your best in school.

Which was also why once she was convinced that you had become a schoolboy above and beyond everything else, nothing she had or could come by was too good for you.

At first (when she was not yet Miss Tee but Auntee) she was mostly the one who always came to cuddle, kiss, and oopdedoopdedoodle you saying Some brown sugarboy lips and some sugarboy brownskin cheekbones and some brown sugarboy foreheadbone and some sugarboy brown right-hand knockout knucklebone and some left-hand knuckle-bone too. May your Anne Tee have some pretty please help herself to some of all this yum yum sugar and all this yum yum honey plus all this buster brownskin pudding and pie.

Then she was also the one who always used to come looking Where is my mister buster brownskin? as soon as she stepped inside the gate, smiling I Spy through her good fairy ring-fingers. Where in the world can he be this time Miss Melba? Oh I think I think I know I think I see guess who Miss Melba. But my how he just keeps on growing and growing so Miss Melba. This is isn't it the same Mister daredevil roustabout I had to look east of the woodpile and west of the hen nest to find last time Miss Melba, and east of the sunflowers west of the kitchen steps the time before that, and east of the east the time before that and west of the west the time before that and north of the north and south of the south the time before that and the time before that.

Then also more often then not: How would you like to may he Miss Melba come play awhile at my house this afternoon? Miss Melba says if you want to wouldn't you like to come visit your Miss Tee and see the new surprise something from the Sears and Roebuck Catalogue My Mister? To which I refuse to remember ever having said no. Not with all the storebought toys she always had both inside the house and out.

You couldn't see where she lived from the chinaberry tree, but as soon as you came to Miss Missie Mae Ferguson's corner all you had to do was turn right and her house was the one with the whitewashed fence and flower garden and green latticework framing the swingporch. And there was also a screened-in back porch with a rocking horse, and in the backyard there were two plowline swings and a see-saw and a playshed that could become a play house, a play store, a play mill, a play school or anything else you wanted it to be.

Her husband was Mister Paul Miles Boykin, but he was not my uncle; not only because she was already my auntee before he came and married her, but also and mainly because I never did like him. I disliked his side-watchful eyes and shiny cowlicks and charlie chaplin mop of a mustache from the very outset, and then one day I also realized that the thing about his voice was that it almost always sounded as if he were trembling without knowing it because he could hardly keep himself from slapping you. That was long before the time he came home and saw me sitting on the back steps eating strawberries and cream and said: That's my money you eating, my young fellow. You don't ever call me your uncle but anytime you asking your Miss Auntee for something you asking Paul Miles Boykin too. When she given you them sailor boy clothes that's my money you wearing, and when you come around here, this my house I'm working and sweating to pay the whitefolks for, and all that's my money you playing with out there in that yard.

Which was also when Miss Tee said: He doesn't know a thing in the world about what's bothering you Mister Boykin. He's only an innocent child Mister Boykin. It's not his fault. If somebody did something wrong I'm the one. To which he said: I'm talking about my money. He also said: I'm talking about if he ain't too innocent to be always coming over here costing me money, he ain't too innocent to start learning a trade. If he was a child of mine I'd be learning him a trade by this time. When I was his age I wasn't setting around on somebody's steps eating no strawberries like money growing on trees. I was already pulling my own row. That's what I'm talking about.

Which is why the very next chance I got I said: What about me when you and Mister Paul Miles get your own little boy Miss Tee? And that was when she said she would always be my Miss Tee and if there were ever a new little boy he would be my cousin and I could always play like he was my little brother.

You always used to know when it was Sunday morning again as soon as you woke up, because everything was always so still and quiet. Then instead of sawmills and lumber trucks and train whistles and switch engines there would be Sunday School bells, which in those days you could hear from churches as far away as Pine Hill Chapel, and which always used to sound as if they were sunshine blue and sunshine yellow even when you were listening through wind and rain.

Then it would be time for my Sunday morning bath before putting on my blue serge Sunday-go-to-meeting suit plus my Buster Brown kneestockings with my tongue-and-sidebuckle lowquarter Buster Brown Shoes plus my silk pongee shirt with my sailorboy bowtie plus my sailorboy blue flat-top hat. (That was when you used Palmolive instead of plain everyday washing soap, and you combed and brushed your hair using Pluko or Poro instead of plain everyday Vaseline, and when there was no Mum, you used to have to rub baking soda under your arms, and sometimes you also had to rub the shine off your nose and cheeks with Mama's chamois skin.)

Then it would be time for Sunday morning breakfast, and sometimes the main thing would be fresh pan sausage with flapjacks and molasses, and at other times it might be pork chops or fried chicken, and in season that was also when you got the best batter-fried oysters with grits and butter. But what I always remember first when I remember how it used to be when company was there for Sunday breakfast is smothered steak plus onion gravy with grits and with biscuits plus your choice of homemade blackberry jelly or peach jam or pear preserve or watermelon rind preserve. Along with all of which there was that special aroma of French Market chickory coffee which I didn't drink in those days but which I still remember when I remember Alabama Sunday mornings as I also remember barbershop cigar smoke when I remember how Saturday mornings used to be.

It was as if the big bells which used to ring for eleven o'clock services were there to hammer silver and gold for the stars and crowns the big choir used to sing about in heavenly host harmony above the stainedglass holiness of the organ. I used to think the pulpit was there because it was the same thing as the throne before which you were going to have to stand and give final testimony on Judgment Day (while all around you the whole world was becoming a lake of fire and brimstone into which the condemned would backslide).

There was also a time when I used to think Miss Sister

Lucinda Wiggins was somebody who was not only trying to go to Heaven whole soul and body like the prophet Elijah, but was indeed over halfway there already, what with the way she always used to sit in the number one seat in the Amen Corner diagonally rocking in double time while fanning herself in half time. Saying: preach the word sir, tell them about it. And then saying: Lord have mercy Lord have mercy on my soul. In such a way as was always certain to move somebody to respond by breaking into one of the moans that she herself had made famous: Lord poor sinner in a hmmmmm aa hmmmmm. Lord the poor sin-ner innnn aaaaa hmmmmmmmm aaaaa hmmmmmmmmm. And what with the way she would then say Yes Jesus yes Jesus yes Jesus yes Lord yes Jesus yes Lord yes Jesus yes Lord.

Sometimes she used to become so full of the Holy Ghost that she used to get up and strut up and down the aisle from the Amen Corner to the deacon's bench (stepping now in half time and fanning in double time) as if she could walk right on into a pillow of smoke and take the chariot to the Chancery on High. But most of the time it was as if she was there because it was her sacred duty to see to it that enough spirit was generated (between the Word and the worshippers) to make somebody else shout. Then when somebody like Miss Big Martha Sanford or Miss Edwina Henry used to start dancing and talking in unknown tongues it was also her duty to nod that it was time to calm them down or take them outside.

You used to have to be there in the midst of all of that (if not every Sunday at least every other Sunday), and sometimes the sermons used to be so full not only of ugly prophecies and warnings but also outright threats of devine vengeance on hyprocrites that when people all around you began stomping and clapping and shouting you couldn't tell whether they were doing so because they were being visited by the Holy Ghost or because being grownfolks and therefore accountable for their trespasses they were even more terrified of the dreadful wrath of God than you were (whose sins after all were still being charged against your parents).

Then when the pastor (who always struck me as being as much God's sheriff as God's shepherd) finally took his seat again, the entire congregation smelling not only of Palmolive soap (or Sweetheart soap or pine tar soap) but also of silk and satin and taffeta and jewelry and cologne and fur pieces and powder-puff bosoms, and of bay rum and talcum plus shoe polish and cigar fingers, used to ruffle-shuffle and stand in unison as if to rise shine and give God their glory by clapping and singing like soldiers of the Cross; and you knew it would not be but so much longer before you would be outside once more and on your way back home to find out what mischief the Katzenjammer Kids were getting into this time.

(Because you were not allowed to look at the Sunday-colored funnypapers in the *Mobile Register*—or the *New Orleans Times-Picayune* until you had first remembered the Sabbath day and kept it holy. But all the same Maggie and Jiggs like Mutt and Jeff and the Katzenjammer Kids used to be as much a part of Sunday as my Sunday School cards.)

Then it would be time for dinner with the Sunday table setting, and sometimes the main dish used to be baked hen with cornbread stuffing, and sometimes it was stewed chicken with dumplings, and sometimes it would be beef roast with brown gravy and mashed potatoes or pork roast with candied yams, and that was also when you had baked smoke-cured ham and potato salad that was almost as good as that which Miss Sister Lucinda Wiggins always made to sell on her church supper plates. And there would be side dishes of turnips and mustards which were more special than everyday collards plus tomatoes and cucumbers and red radishes, and for very very special occasions brown edged garden lettuce quick-smothered in olive oil and vinegar.

But the most special Sunday treat of all was ice cream. Not even those banquet festive times when you were permitted to help yourself to a hunk of jelly layer cake plus a slice of sweet potato pie plus a slice of coconut custard pie on the same serving were better than those Sundays on which by cracking the ice and turning the freezer you earned the right to scrape the dasher all by yourself. Unless there were so many for company that all had to be served at dinnertime, Mama always used to save one last smidgen until everybody got back after the Sunday night sermon, and then the only thing left over would be the wooden freezer bucket of melting ice on the dark summer gallery, plus the burlap-fuzzy aftertaste of ice cream salt as you fell off to sleep.

Then it would be Monday morning again, and I would hear Mama (who unlike Miss Sister Lucinda Wiggins was never one to make even the slightest display of her religious devotion in public) wake up saying what I always knew were her prayers and I would know that she was beginning another week by making thankful acknowledgement to a jealous but ever so merciful Heavenly Master that it was by His infinite and amazing Grace that creatures such as we in all our pitiful unworthiness were still spared to be here to be numbered among the living—which was the first Blessing, from which all other blessings flow.

Then, more often than not (because the chances were that you had dozed back off in the meantime) the next thing you heard would be her humming to herself in the kitchen; and what she would be humming was most likely to be either a prayer meeting hymn or an Amen Corner moan. In any case I don't remember Mama ever singing the actual words of any verses that early in the day.

But sometimes you might hear her mumbling something to herself precisely because she was praying again. And sometimes that was also when she used to talk as if to herself but really to the Maker, about the headlong and headstrong sinfulness of this day and time in this His world now so offensive to His majestical sight, who glory unto His holy name, had only to lift His little finger and wipe out all creation.

That was one way you could tell when she was either somewhat bothered or downright troubled about something. And sometimes she used to talk as if directly to God the Father (who sometimes listened from the low hanging clouds or from a sunbeam or perhaps even from a breeze against the windowpanes, and in His own good time answered—sometimes with raging thunder and lightning and sometimes with smiling flowers and bountiful fruit).

So Monday morning was also the time when you were most likely to hear Mama quoting from the Bible, saying: You said thus and so and thus and so Lord and I believe; and You said so forth and so on and I believe, because Father I do believe.

Monday morning was also when Miss Sister Lucinda Wiggins used to wake up sometimes with so much leftover Sunday spirit and Holy Ghost that she had to tell the whole wide world about it. That was when you could sit in the chinaberry tree and see the smoke from her washpot in her backyard on the corner of Gins Alley and Cross Street and hear her moaning at the rub board as if for the benefit of the neighborhood at large. Then sometimes the next thing used to be Miss Libby Lee Tyler answering from her backyard at this end of Gins Alley; and the two of them would begin singing and humming back and forth at each other, and before long somebody else would join in (sometimes somebody like Miss Edwina Henry from as far away as half way to the AT & N on Cross Street) and sometimes by the time they were all ready to hang out their first batch of white pieces it was as if they were having a community wide Monday morning prayer meeting.

Nothing makes me remember Miss Sister Lucinda Wiggins and Miss Libby Lee Tyler and all that so much as when two trumpet players begin trading blues choruses on an up-tempo dance arrangement, with the trombones and saxophones moaning and shouting in the background. Because that was also what I used to think about back when Little Buddy Marshall and I used to stand outside the Masonic Temple (or the Boon Men's Union Hall Ballroom) after a baseball game or a picnic listening to Sonny Tarver and Dewitt Ellis blowing back and forth at each other in Daddy Gladstone Giles' Excelsior Marching and Social Band.

Not that I didn't always know that the one thing you were never likely to hear Mama, Miss Sister Lucinda Wiggins or any other church folks humming, mumbling, to say nothing of singing, or even listening to at any time whatsoever back in those days was blues music. And no wonder either. Because according to every preacher or deacon who ever mentioned it the blues was the music of the Devil. When you said you had the blues (which was exactly the same as saying that the blues had you) that was only another way of saying that you were so possessed of sin that your soul was already churning in torment.

Because according to every preacher and Sunday School teacher I can remember, the reason you were not supposed to wake up with the blues was simple enough: once you were converted from the ways of sinfulness to the truth of the light you were supposed to have acquired soul salvation, which meant nothing if not precisely that you were saved not only from the fiery furnaces of the red Devil himself, but also from his ever busy imps the plain old everyday blue devils that bedeviled the world with the temptations of the flesh only to double right back and trouble your conscience to desolation and despair—which of course was, so far as church folks were concerned, all too obviously what singing the blues (by which they really meant crying the blues) was all about in the first place.

Not that you were not brought up in terms of all of that. But even so what I myself almost always used to think blues music was mostly about when I used to hear Luzana Cholly playing his notorious silver stringed gold fretted pearl studded guitar was not fire and brimstone but the blue steel train whistle blueness of the briarpatch (the habitat

97

not only of the booger bear whose job was to frighten naughty children into obedience but also of that most grizzly and terrifying of all bears, the one who according to fireside and barbershop accounts put the mug on you, ripped out the seat of your pants and made you a tramp, ripped off the soles of your shoes, wiped out crops and caused famines, shut down mills and factories and caused panics.)

Nor were all church folks always as hard set against blues music when it came to Luzana Cholly as most of their remarks would otherwise lead you to expect. Because on occasion even Mama and Uncle Jerome used to forget. Because sometimes when he used to come strumming his way up out of the L & N bottom while we were all sitting on the front gallery in the summer twilight, Mama would be the very first one to say: There come old box-picking Luzana Cholly playing the fool out of that old thing like nobody else in the world. With never a word about him being on his way either to or from a skin game, or to a jook house. And Uncle Jerome would clear his throat and say: Old Luzana Cholly. Old Luzana Cholly out there amongst them. That's him all right. Here he come and ain't no two ways about it. Old Luzana Cholly. I done told you.

When it came to old frizzly headed, wicked walking, sneaky looking Stagolee Dupas (fils) however, and the kind of music he used to play on the piano, church folks used to call it the low-down dirty blues even when it was not. Because old Stagolee (who so far as Little Buddy Marshall and I were concerned was to honed steel and patent leather what old Luzana Cholly was to blue steel and rawhide) was liable to barrelhouse you right on out into the black alley in the simple process of vamping the chords to "Nearer My God to Thee."

Mister Stagolee Dupas (fils), or the Stagolee Kid was also called Stagolee the Son of Stagolee and Stagolee the Younger and Stagolee Junior and Son Stag and Kid Stag not because he was the son of the original Mister Bad Bad Stagolee (who was sometimes referred to as old Trigger Fingered Stagolee) but because he had followed in the footsteps of and probably even surpassed his father (who was a piano player famous for making up verses about the original Bad Man Stagolee, the notorious gambler who packed a stack barrel Forty-four). Sometimes when Stagolee the Son of Stagolee used to start adding some of his own new verses, he would keep on going until he had a verse for every key on the piano.

Mister Stagolee Dupas (fils) with his Creole pirate's mustache and his Creole bayou sideburns and his New Orleans sporting house patent leather shoes and his gambling den silk shirts. Not to mention the indescribably wicked way he had of winking at women without really winking at all, which was something he was almost as notorious for as for the way he also used to walk his left hand right on into the dirty dozens while keeping his own special til-the-cows-come-home tremolo going on and on with his right until (as somebody was forever repeating) the king of the signifying monkeys was subject to be out of tales to tell and out of breath to boot.

There were also long gone freight train whistles in the music he used to play years before anybody started calling

that kind of blues boogie-woogie and he could also play
wedding music and the church organ. But the only thing
you were ever likely to hear any church folks mention him
for was Saturday Night Music, which they also called Good
Time Music, by which they meant the kind of nightlong
blues-dragging, blues-rocking, blues-bumping, blues-jump-
ing, blues-swinging, blues-shouting music for Saturday night
honky tonk dances during which, according to them, somebody was forever getting stabbed or cutup or shotup and
ending up either in the hospital or the graveyard, with
somebody else either skipping city or going to jail and then
on to the County Farm or the chain gang.

Because the word on him among most church folks was
always the same: He had not only come from hell and was
on his way back to there, but was indeed so obviously in
league with the Devil that he had turned up in Gasoline
Point precisely because he had been dispatched special
delivery from the dins and dives of sin ridden New Orleans
for the express purpose for providing all but irresistible
wickedness for the weak and temptation for backsliders.

You could always count on somebody preaching another
fire and brimstone sermon about the ungodly good time
music in the houses of doom and iniquity whenever there
had been another one of the sheriff's raids on the honky
tonks, and the following Monday morning you could also
count on hearing Miss Sister Lucinda Wiggins again. But
what she used to tell the world when it was that kind of
Monday morning was not about how the Comforter had
come and brought joy joy joy to her soul, but about trouble
in the land.

Sometimes when you heard somebody singing something other than church music over in Gins Alley on Monday morning it used to be Miss Honey Houston, whose house was next door to Miss Pauline's Cookshop, and who always used to begin with the same opening verse: Going to see Madame Ruth/Going to see Madame Catherine/Going to tell Madame Ruth/Going tell Madame Catherine (Got a world full of trouble/And sweet daddy so doggone mean).

But the one I remember above everybody else when I remember somebody who used to wake up on Monday morning and let the whole neighborhood know that she had another bad case of the blues, no matter what all the preachers and church folks in the state of Alabama said, is Miss Blue Eula Bacote who used to live at the other end of Gins Alley in the house with the yard that was mostly a flower garden and always used to wear high-heel patent leather pumps and spang-dangling 18-carat gold earrings with her almost-frizzly hair bobbed and poroed like a big city flapper, and used to have the best short plump brown-skin strut you ever saw, even when she was too drunk to do anything except flash her jewel-studded Gay Paree cigarette holder.

The first thing she always used to do (after lighting a cigarette and making coffee) was wind up her Victrola and put on the latest record of Bessie Smith singing the blues. Then she would open all the doors and windows. And then she used to move all of the furniture out into the clean-swept part of the yard and string all of her hangers of coats, suits and frocks on the clothesline, and spread the mattress ticking and stuffing on the grass and drape all of her quilts and blankets on the fence. Then she used to get down on her knees with a scrubbing brush and a bucket of hot sudsy lye water and do all of the floors plus the porch and the steps.

Sometimes she used to play the same Bessie Smith record over and over and sometimes all you used to hear would be Bessie Smith and Ma Rainey. But most of the time she also used to like to listen to Mamie Smith and Trixie Smith and Ida Cox, all of whom she always went to see in person in the vaudeville every time they came to Mobile to play at the Pike Theatre out on Davis Avenue. And she was also the one who always used to buy every Jelly Roll Morton and King Oliver and Louis Armstrong record as soon as it came out. (So no wonder all of old Louis' highest trumpet runs always seem to come from beyond the roof tops of Gins Alley and to be aimed at me in the chinaberry tree.)

Then while the house was drying and airing out she always used to work on her flowers with the music still playing, and after that she used to sit in her rocking chair sometimes in the shade and sometimes in the sunshine still listening, but now also smoking and drinking black coffee (sometimes darning, sometimes making quilt patches, sometimes shelling peas or beans). But she herself never used to sing or even hum. All she ever used to do was hold her head to one side with her eyes closed and pat her feet and snap her fingers every now and then. The only words I can remember ever hearing her say while the music was playing were Hello central hello central hello central ring me Western Union. Which is what she also used to say on those Saturday nights when she used to sit all by herself in the corner of Sodawater's honky tonk getting high while Mister Mule Bacote, whose real name was Lemuel Bacote but who was also called Eula's Mule, was out in Skin Game Jungle.

Then by midday you wouldn't hear anything else, and

if you went that way going to the post office you wouldn't see her anywhere either, so I always used to think she was probably taking a nap on a pallet in one of the empty rooms. Then by the middle of the afternoon, she always used to start putting everything back in place, and by time to begin supper it was as if she had finally gotten everything ready to make it through another week, and by the time Mister Lem the Mule, who was the number one raft towing expert for Buckshaw Mill, used to get back from the river it was always as if it all had been only another day.

According to most of the backfence and pumpshed mention, speculation and insinuation I used to hear, Miss Eula Bacote came to be the way she was because she was doomed to be forever childless and in love with a good man who was always gambling his hard earned wages away. But the first and foremost thing that comes to mind when I remember her now is how music used to sound on the old wind-up Gramophones of that time. Then what I always see again (along with her stylish clothes) is her yard with all the flowers plus the porch with the trellis and all the planting pots and boxes that used to make me think about Miss Tee every time I used to go through Gins Alley on my way to the kite pasture or the post office.

The music I remember when I remember how Bea Ella
Thornhill came to be known as Miss Red Ella is the special
ragtime piano-roll version of the ever popular oldtime bar-
room ballad about what Frankie did to Johnny that Stagolee Dupias (fils) used to have to play again every time
somebody else in Sodawater MacFadden's jook joint used
to say Hey how about some more mean red evil for the old
boll weevil.

Because not only was the chain of events leading up to
that particular bloody mess a story in itself, it was also one
that almost everybody in Gasoline Point (including me and
Little Buddy Marshall this time) knew or should have
known verse by verse, chorus by chorus and therefore step
by step already. And so also because for the next six or

*seven months following the funeral (to which Bea Ella
came in handcuffs) and that trial (at which she was sentenced to serve a year and a day) it was as if the only thing
left for anybody to do was go and get Stagolee Dupas (fils)
to repeat that long since familiar tune at least four or five
times every Saturday night.*

❂

That day when Little Buddy Marshall and I heard the
screaming and saw people running toward it from every
direction and followed them on up into the alley off the
crape myrtle lane behind Stranahan's store where we saw
what had happened to Beau Beau Weaver neither of us was
in the least surprised by what we heard from those who
were standing there grunting and wagging their heads at
each other as they waited for the sheriff and the coroner.

But then whenever anything which meant serious
trouble of any kind whatsoever happened in Gasoline Point
there was always somebody whose immediate reaction was
to repeat the same old claim: I told you so. I told you so. I
told you so. Even when what had occurred was obviously not
only an accident but one which nobody in that part of the
world at that time was likely either to have seen or even to
have heard of before, somebody had to say it in one way or
another: See there, what did I tell you? What else did you
—could you or anybody else expect?

Even when it was some altogether natural phenomenon
such as, say, a Gulf Coast gale ripping in from the river
and Mobile Bay, you could be absolutely positive that
somebody was somewhere shaking his head and grumbling

as if anybody with any common sense at all should have been able to foresee and if not avert or avoid it at least be better prepared to withstand it.

You could also be every bit as certain that somebody was going to be explaining the fundamental cause along with the overall effect of whatever it was by citing the unimpeachable authority of the Bible. Nor was it at all unusual for somebody else to be pontificating about the natural as well as the human implications of it all with overtones suggestive not only of prophecy, but also of fortunetelling and even in not a few instances of conjuration.

As far as Little Buddy Marshall and I were concerned, however, almost all statements of that nature were likely to have much more to do with such foresight as is inevitably inherent in (and indeed is perhaps inseparable from) all accurate pragmatic insight than with any operation whatsoever—traditional or otherwise—of clairvoyance per se.

In this case the likelihood of a bloody mess had been mentioned more than once, to be sure—but so, as a matter of fact, had a number of other eventualities. But still and all, much more had been said about what had already come to pass in similar circumstances than about what was in store for the one at issue, whether sooner or later. Because what most people were really saying was I seen situations like this seen them time and again and ain't no telling what's going to happen!

Not that anyone we knew ever considered prediction, or perhaps better still, projection to be irrelevant. It was very much to the point indeed. For the moment involves anticipation as well as memory, and action itself is of its very nature nothing if not the most obvious commitment to the future. But if like me and Little Buddy you had been as profoundly conditioned by the twelve-string guitar insinuations of Luzana Cholly and the honky-tonk piano of

Stagolee Dupas (fils) as by anything you had ever heard or overheard in church at school by the fireside or from any other listening post, you knew very well that anything, whether strange or ordinary, happening in Gasoline Point was, in the very nature of things, also part and parcel of the same old briarpatch, which was the same old blue steel network of endlessly engaging and frequently enraging mysteries and riddling ambiguities which encompass all the possibilities and determine all the probabilities in the world. But you also knew something else: no matter how accurate your historical data, no matter how impressive your statistics, the application of experience to flesh-and-blood behavior must always leave something to chance and circumstance.

But then the fact that Luzana Cholly and Stagolee Dupas (fils) were road-seasoned gamblers who were almost as notorious for being footloose ramblers as for playing music was as important to me and Little Buddy as anything else. Because after all if you had been bred and born in the briarpatch, and if like me and him you were enroute to Philamayork you had to be nimble by habit not only like Jack the Rabbit but also like Jack the Bear who could even be nowhere when necessary precisely because having been everywhere he knew when you were supposed to play drunk or even dead. Anyway, you were never supposed to take anything for granted.

Nor had we. And yet nobody, not even those who had always insisted irrevocably that anything under the sun could happen had included what was clearly the most decisive detail of all: Bea Ella Thornhill flashing a switchblade knife. Bea Ella Thornhill flashing a switchblade knife of her own. Bea Ella Thornhill flashing a switchblade knife which she herself had ordered COD from Sears Roebuck three weeks before. Nobody's conjectures had included anything like that at all. Not even after she had been given up as a lost ball in the high weeds.

On the other hand there was neither consternation nor even mild surprise at what had befallen Beau Beau Weaver, who was also known as Bo as in bo'hog and bo'weevil, whose name was Emmett James Scott Weaver but who sometimes bragged about being the weaverer, meaning spell weaver. Because although speculation about him may have been prudently vague, it had always been ominous. It had always included the possibility of violence because what people had expressed most concern about was not his integrity as was the case with Bea Ella Thornhill but his prospects for simple physical survival.

I myself knew that opinion about that had been negative (and unanimous) from the very outset. Because I could remember the day he arrived from the piney woods of Mississippi. I was the one who saw him when he got off the turpentine trailer at the AT & N crossing carrying a cardboard suitcase. I was the one who told him where the boarding house was.

Most people had registered serious misgivings about him as soon as they saw how he was dressed and the kind of airs he was putting on when he came breezing onto the block that first Saturday at twilight. And everything he said and did thereafter only substantiated their initial impressions. But as soon as the nature of his association with Bea Ella Thornhill became common knowledge, all speculations and conjectures began to seem like foregone conclusions.

So there was some justification for saying I told you so about what had happened to Beau Beau Weaver. But even as we stood there in the blood-stained green plus honeysuckle-yellow alleyway conceding that much, Little Buddy and I also remembered that beneath the consensus of open-ended forebodings we had always detected as much wishful thinking as understanding of the nature of consequence, inevitability or even of cause and effect. Because what most of them had been talking about had far less to do with the inscrutable than with their own theories about the wages of sin.

Because what had really been bothering people more than anything else was the fact that a schoolgirl like Bea Ella Thornhill who was every bit as good looking as Creola Calloway, for instance, but who had always been as sweet and well-mannered and *promising* as Creola Calloway was outrageous—had not only run away from her guardian—(and set up housekeeping with Beau Beau Weaver of all people) but had also hired herself out as a maid for white people as if she had never even been near a school—not to mention knowing how to record minutes and keep books. That was scandalous enough in itself but to top it off, all she did with the money she made was let him spend it on himself. That was certainly one reason they forgot about her even in the process of putting the bad mouth on him. It was as if the worst had happened to her already.

Most of what Little Buddy and I had learned about what people began calling Bea Ella's boll weevil epidemic situation had come from barbershop talk. But the very first time I had heard anything at all about it was not in the barbershop, but one day at the pump shed when Aunt Callie the Cat was talking to Miss Liza Jefferson about it. I was pumping wash water for Miss Liza Jefferson that day and Aunt Callie who was working in her front yard flower garden, came catting out to the fence in her unlaced man's brogans to give Miss Liza some cuttings from her famous rose trellis, and as usual they started swapping the news and Aunt Callie had the main items.

But Lord, she said as soon as they got through pretending that neither had heard any new gossip. Somebody did tell me Bea Ella Thornhill done taken up with that old low-down, good-looking nasty walking, sweet-smelling, grand rascal of a Bo Weaver or whatever his name is.

No she ain't neither, Miss Liza Jefferson said, shaking her head as if that would somehow keep it from having already happened.

That's what they tell me.

Aw you gone on now, Cat. You know good and well Bea Ella ain't done that. You know that child as well as I do.

If it's a lie it ain't mine, honey.

Well, I am speechless, honey, I'm just plain speechless. I just flat cain't open my mouth.

Lord, Beau Weaver, Jesus.

They tell me he a bo-weaver all right.

Mamie was telling me.

Mamie Taylor? Lord, Father in heaven, I ain't seen Mamie Taylor since I don't know when. When have I seen Mamie Taylor, Jesus?

Mamie say it happened right up there at that church supper the other night.

Up in Lula Crayton's yard. You know something? I plain forgot all about that until I suddenly got to wondering where everybody was, and it was too late to go then.

Mamie Taylor say he was there standing around looking just like he just stepped out of a bandbox as usual and after a while he sided up to that child's table and bought a plate of supper and stood there talking and eating and then he bought another one and ate that and stayed there laughing and talking, and stayed right on there and by that time he had her laughing and talking too, and when it come time to go they left together.

Now you know that gal ought to know better than that.

Lord, that grand rascal'll have that child so she don't know her head from her heels.

And after that I heard some others talking about it too, Miss Ida Thompson for instance, and Miss Millie Chapman; and every now and then Mama would be talking about it too; and I even heard Hot Water Shorty Hollingsworth telling Stagolee's Vyola that it was a pity and a shame that Bea Ella had been saving herself and her reputation all that time just to throw it all away for nothing on the likes of somebody who didn't stand for any more than Beau Weaver stood for.

But the main source of information that Little Buddy and I had about subjects like that and a number of other things as well in those days was Papa Gumbo Willie McWorthy's barbershop, because during that time, which was not long after old Jaycee Dickenson went to Kansas City, we didn't have to wait until we needed a haircut in order to be there. Because the new shoeshine expert who later on was going to become a chauffeur and a mechanic for Lem Buckshaw of Buckshaw Mill Company family and leave for Seattle, Washington was old Cateye Gander Gallagher whom everybody knew had always been our number one big buddy.

All you had to do was stop by as if you had come only because you wanted to watch old Cateye holding his head to one side like a drummer, skip popping a patent leather finish on somebody's Edwin Clapps. Not that you had anybody fooled. That was simply the way you had to do it. And when they started talking about something like, say, sporting houses such as those in New Orleans and San

Francisco, or say the shysters, pimps and streetwalkers who hung out in Pig Alley which was in Paris, France, they were only pretending that they had forgotten that you were there listening because somebody had decided that it was time for you to start hearing about something like that.

Whenever that happened, as it did the day I heard old Soldierboy Crawford answering questions about such Parisian curiosities as pissoirs and bidets and then best of all, talking about getting paid to be in a smutty postcard show with three French women wearing frog stockings, somebody would also slip in something about the kind of diseases you had to know about but were not yet old enough to ask grown people about.

Everybody knew exactly what you were doing there, and all you were supposed to do was stay quiet and listen. And then finally somebody like old Davenport Davis, for instance, would turn and say, Boy you still here? Boy, you heard all that? Well if you cunning enough to get away with that I reckon, goddammit, you also clever enough to know you supposed to keep it to yourself. You go round repeating this stuff you ain't going to show nobody how much you know. All you going to do is show how much you don't know about when to keep your mouth shut.

Hell I'm satisfied he know that, Papa Gumbo Willie McWorthy, himself also said. And there was something about the way he winked when he said it that made me realize that Mama and Papa were no less satisfied because it was suddenly as plain as day to me that they were in on the whole thing too.

It was from the barbershop that I learned the all important differences between ordinary high yallers whose parents were high yallers, and brand new mulattoes. And it was also in the barbershop that I found out that Elmore Collins had left so suddenly for Los Angeles, California because there was no way in the world for the white people in Tucker's Quarters not to realize what had been going on between him and Miss Jessica Butterfield when one of them happened to be taking a shortcut through her peach orchard and saw him coming out of her backyard at 4:30 A.M. and her watching him from the backroom window.

Boy, Miss Jessica Butterfield don't count because she is one in a minnion. She can do anything she want to because she can buy every peckerwood in Tucker's Quarters. Buy them and bale them. Boy it's them others you got to worry about. Because just remember when they start looking at you they can holler rape if you don't and if you do you can be damn sure that's what they going holler if you get caught. And they'll know she lying and come after you just the same. Boy, Miss Jessica Butterfield hid her sweet nigger out, give him his get-away money and walked down the middle of the goddamn street with a goddamn silk poker dot umbrella and don't even have to think about daring a single one of them bad-assed peckerwoods to even whisper. Boy that's one widow woman can lift her little pink ring finger and shut down half this town and starve every peckerwood in sight.

It was Papa Gumbo Willie McWorthy's barbershop and he was there most of the time but he was not a barber himself. He was an old Mississippi riverboat cook and he had also been a bartender in a San Francisco gambling den. Now he was a businessman and most of the time he sat at the cash register when he was not at the cookshop which he owned next door. He was called Papa because he had traveled so much and had seen and done so many things. But to this day I still don't know whether he was called Papa Gumbo because he knew so many Creole recipes or because his feet were as flat as gunboats.

The top barber at that time was Vanderbilt Coleman

who had once been a pullman porter on the Southern Pacific. He was the one who was always talking about what was going on in the newspaper, and his Bible was the World Almanac. He always wore white Van Heusen shirts (some with collars and some without) and his tan shoes were the handmade kind that shine more and more like antique brass as the instep darkens.

The number one expert on big league baseball was Eddie Ashley who had a collection of Reach and Spaulding guide books which went all the way back to 1913. The best checkers players were Decatur Callahan who was also a trombone player, and Chee Cholly Middleton who worked at Chickasaw dry docks and who was just as good when he came in as the money ball relief pitcher backing up old Stringbean Henderson as when he was playing third base.

But the one who almost always turned out to have most of the latest inside news about what was going on in Gasoline Point whenever the talk got around to the subject of men and women was Otis Smedley who in addition to being a jack leg carpenter and handyman was also the one who was always sought after by Baptist, Methodist and sanctified refreshment committees alike during picnics, camp meetings and association time because when it came to making barbecue and Brunswick stew everybody agreed that nobody could touch him. Anyway, Otis Smedley was the one who knew most about what had been going on all along between Beau Beau Weaver and Bea Ella Thornhill.

I was not there the day he told about what happened that time when Beau Beau took her up to Miss Clementee Mayberry's boarding house. But old Gander Gallagher passed it on to me and Little Buddy when we saw him in Gins Alley after work that same night. Nobody really knew where Otis Smedley got his account from, but when he told

114

it everybody believed it and they could only assume that he had heard it from Beau Beau Weaver himself.

Beau Beau had nice-talked her for three weeks and finally got her to go and she knew exactly what she was going for. But when she got there and it came time for to pull her clothes off she made him go into the closet and when she let him come back in she was standing not by the bed but in the middle of the room all wrapped up in the top sheet with her eyes closed as tight as she could get them and when he began unwinding it she started moaning and praying, saying Jesus forgive me, over and over.

Beau Beau's main hangout, the main place to look for him, was the poolroom, but he also used to come by the barbershop two or three times a week. The first thing he always did was have his shoes shined, and then he would stand primping before the mirror and if he decided that he didn't need his English brushback touched up he would help himself to the lotions and creams, whisk himself down and then flip Vanderbilt Coleman a two-bit tip.

Sometimes, of course, everybody would act is if he were not even there, let alone being noticed; to which he would respond by humming to himself and prancing around as if he were alone in his own private dressing room. Then he would hunch his sides with his elbows and breeze on out whistling through his teeth.

But as often as not somebody would start signifying at him about, say, where he was getting so many fancy clothes from and you could see that he was pleased because he really thought everybody in Gasoline Point was envious of him. He also assumed that everybody regarded him as being such a sweet man that women were climbing all over each other to get to him and to be sure that is what some few who didn't know any better actually did assume.

What those in the barbershop were really signifying about most of the time, however, was the rumor that the reason he didn't have to work in the daytime was not that so many women wanted to take care of him, since so far as anybody knew only Bea Ella Thornhill went that far, but because he worked at night delivering whiskey to the white-folks' roadhouses for a white bootlegger from Leakesville, Mississippi. You could not tell that he ever suspected that part at all. Because all he would do was wink and grin and start signifying right back at them.

Ain't nothing to me, man.

Man who you stuffing?

I wouldn't stuff you, cousin.

What you putting down, sweet boy?

Tracks, daddy, just bird tracks. And that ain't many.

Just listen at him.

I ain't saying nothing, home boy.

Boy, all I can say is I just wish I had your line. That's all I can say.

Now just listen at him.

Just look at them dry goods all homes is wearing.

These just some of my working clothes, horse collar.

You hear him, Bander Bill?

I hear him.

And he ain't lying either.

Where you working nowadays, Beauboy Pretty?

Now watch out there now, pudding.

Boy they tell me you working all over this man's town, and I know what kind of work, too.

Now see there. Now there you go. That's the kind of old stuff you got to watch, sweetings.

Boy, if I had your hand, I'd throw mine in. That's all I say.

He would be standing his ever-so-cute pigeon-toed stand by the door then, smiling like he was almost blushing and sometimes he would be talking in a back-at-you wolfing voice and sometimes he would be flashing his diamond ring with a cigarette in his hand and talking airish talk and getting it all mixed up, like saying are for *is* and *doesn't* for *don't* and *knew* for *knowed* and *came* for *come* and even adding words like *psychological* and *financial transaction*, and *incomprehensibility* and *ignorance personified*; and sometimes when he got ready to leave he would announce that he was regretfully making his departure from such an informational educational and inspirational but uneconomical vicinity and that he would recapitulate around that way again whenever his business permitted his absence to that recreational extent and degree.

Then through the plate glass window you could see him pausing outside by the barber's pole making sure that his hat was blocked long, the brim turned up Birmingham style. Then with his left shoulder hunched up and his left arm hanging loose he would move on off down the sidewalk toward Stranahan's block doing his wide tipping pigeon-toed walk about which Little Buddy who liked it even less than I did, used to say: Sheeet man, that ain't no goddamn mammy-hunching patent leather walk. Sheeet, look at that countryfied granny dodger. Think he so sporty and all he doing is looking like his goddamn feet killing him, like he got to pick them up and shake them and let his corns and bunions get some air everytime he take a goddamn step.

And even trying to get some of old Stagolee's slow dragging limp in it so somebody will think he got so many women they wearing him down. Sheeet, hell, goddamn, he just got the goddamn backache from handling all them whiskey jugs. Sheeet everybody know the only good-looking stuff he don't have to pay for is Bea Ella and she don't count. Sheeet, I bet you Creola wouldn't even look at that country-ass sapsucker—goddamn!

He had been in that barbershop the same morning. He had come in whistling to himself to let everybody know that he was in a hurry to get his primping done so he could be on his way to what was obviously a very special rendezvous. But as soon as he got to the mirror the signifying had begun with Chee Cholly Middleton and Decatur Callahan wolfing back and forth at each other without even looking up from the checkerboard.

Man I can't help it. Man don't pay me no mind.

You hear him don't you Papa Gums. Remember this now.

Man I can't help it if some can and some can't. Man, some got it and some ain't.

Y'all hear him now.

Man you don't have to hear me. Man all you got to do is see me. See me coming raise your window high . . . see me leaving, hang your nappy nit-picking head and cry. I'm just passing by, man.

Well, me myself I'm just plain old everyday Cooter Callahan. Don't go to be no nighthawk and nothing like that. But that's all right. I'm still subject to touch you one of these times. Just don't let me put my finger on you in none of these alleys one night. Just be sure I don't walk right up and put my dog finger on you, horse collar.

You and Otis Smedley, huh.

Me and Otis Smedley? What about me and the law?

He had not been gone for more than an hour when we heard the first screams. Then we saw the people and then we were running to catch them, and what we found when we got there was him lying sprawled in nothing but his underwear and socks, cut to death.

Then we saw Bea Ella too. She was sitting on Miss Clementee's front steps with her hands in her lap as if they had already put the handcuffs on her. She was saying nothing, doing nothing and looking at nothing.

The first screams, it turned out, were those of Earlene Barlow, who had jumped out of the window with nothing on except her underskirt and struck off across toward Good Hope Baptist Church and the carline, running for everything she was worth. So by the time even the first of us got there she was probably somewhere over in Buckshaw Mill Quarters or half way to Blue Poplar Swamp.

Miss Clementee had been screaming too, but she had quieted down because she was the one who was there telling about it, saying: Lord Jesus, Bea Ella didn't say a mumbling word. Not a mumbling word. Beauboy and Earlene Barlow was there in that room and before anybody realized anything Bea Ella was already in the house and down the hall and bambing at the door where they was. That was when Earlene sailed out through the window.

That must have been when Miss Clementee herself started screaming because she said the next thing she saw was Bea Ella with the knife in her hand: And Lord, him trying to back away from her down the hall trying to soft-talk her then her swiping and stabbing at him with all her might. He was pleading with her then, but she still wasn't saying anything. She was not cursing and not crying, but she was not slacking up one bit either.

He was dodging and scrambling backwards all the time and she missed him all the way down the hall, but he got hung up in the screen door and that was where she stuck him the first time. That was when Miss Clementee started trying to call for somebody to come and help. But it was too late then. Because it was happening too fast then. Because he was staggering across the porch and down the steps and she was right after him, and all he could say was No baby, No baby, trying to ward her off with the hand he wasn't holding himself with.

She got him all hemmed up in the gate then, and it looked like she was going crazy cutting him, and by that time he couldn't help himself at all. And by the time the first people got there it was all over. He had finally torn himself out of the gate and started down the lane and had fallen right where he was now.

As for Bea Ella all she did then was drop the knife and stumble back to Miss Clementee's steps and sit there just staring out in front of her with her hands bloody and blood all up and down the front of her dress.

We were all there then, and I saw the rest of it myself, which was him lying there twisted and dead in the ragged shade of the honeysuckle lane, and her just sitting by herself on the boarding house steps waiting to give herself up to the law.

He must have fallen forward because his forehead and chest were not only bloody but also smeared with grit, but somehow or other he had rolled himself partly over on his right side and turned his head almost face up. There was a deep gash that ran all the way from his ear to the corner of his mouth. His right arm was doubled up under him, but his left hand was still clutching his private parts, because the lower part of his stomach had been ripped open, and his very insides were hanging out.

He must have been stabbed and cut in almost a dozen different places on his arms and the upper part of his body alone. His silk undershirt was just a mess of blood and sand and rips, and there was I don't know how much blood puddled under him, especially under his waist. There was so much there that it was as dark and sticky thick-looking as fresh liver, and there was something grayish white oozing from his bowels and there was water still dripping from his bladder too.

We stood waiting for the sheriff and the coroner to get there, and Miss Clementee Mayberry was telling it over and over and saying: Lord, I didn't know what to do. I just didn't know what to do, saying Lord this and Lord Jesus that as almost all grown people in Gasoline Point almost always did on such occasions. It was only afterwards that you thought about which ones were the church members and which were not.

Then that part was over. The coroner had released the body to Windham and Borders Funeral Home. Bam Buchanan was on his way back to Mobile County Jail carrying Bea Ella Thornhill whose only statement had been: Yes, I did. Miss Clementee Mayberry had been taken back into the boarding house. The place had been raked to bury the blood, and as the crowd broke up, what was being said was all about Beau Beau Weaver and none of it was essentially different from anything which everybody had been saying all along, except that now that an ugly fate had been witnessed as an accomplished fact, the tone of scandal and outrage which had marked the months of anticipation had become softened to one of shame and pity.

But when Little Buddy and I got back to the barber-shop Vanderbilt Coleman was saying that Bea Ella Thornhill was the one people should be thinking about, not Beau Beau Weaver. Because all you were talking about when that had happened to him was the Law of Averages, and nothing anybody said about that was going to make any difference anymore anyway. She was the one who was going to have to suffer the consequences of murder, the least of which was the prison term.

That was when Papa Gumbo Willie McWorthy called it red murder, and that was how Bea Ella Thornhill became Red Ella from then on, which seemed to make most people remember seeing her streaked with blood sitting alone on the boarding house steps waiting to confess. But Little Buddy and I knew that Papa Gumbo Willie McWorthy had said red because what he was really talking about was the blues. Because he was responding to what Vanderbilt Coleman had said was Bea Ella Thornhill's biggest mistake of all: Not knowing that bad luck and disappointment meant not the end of the world but only that being human you had to suffer like everybody else from time to time.

So what he was actually describing was a woman seeing red but feeling nothing. And when she came back from County Farm not only acting like a middle-aged church widow but also looking and even walking like one it was as if she had been sentenced to serve a year and a day in prison and had been paroled to spend the rest of her life either bent over a sewing machine or floating along in a trance. Anyway, from then on she was Miss Red Ella and she always smiled at you as if she were seeing you through a red crepe veil; and no matter who said what—or what you were telling or asking her about, she always made the same reply, which to her was obviously the last word on everything: God doesn't love ugly and doesn't care too much about pretty either.

Sometimes Stagolee Dupas used to spend the whole afternoon alone at the piano in the empty dancing room of Sodawater's honky tonk playing for nobody but himself. That was when he used to sit patting his left foot and running blues progressions by the hour, touching the keys as gently as if he could actually feel the grain of each note with his finger tips, sustaining each chord and listening with his right ear cocked (and his right shoulder sloped) as if to give it time to soak all the way into the core of his very being. When all you could hear was the piano he was probably thinking up new blues ballad verses, because when you heard his voice when he was alone like that he was not singing lyrics but humming all the instrumental fills, riffs and solo take-off to himself as if he were a one man band.

Then sometimes he used to spend the next two or three hours playing sheet music, including such new and recent tunes as "Ain't She Sweet," "Three Little Words," "Lilac Time," and "My Blue Heaven," which I used to whistle to myself almost as much as I used to whistle "Sundown," "Little White Lies," "Precious Little Thing Called Love," and "Dream a Little Dream of Me" (which I still find myself whistling to myself this many years later anytime anything really takes me back to those days when I was the schoolboy I used to be and used to feel the way I used to feel about some of the honey brown girls I used to know).

There were also times when what he used to follow the blues with would be ragtime tunes (some of which he used to play note for note as you heard them on the piano rolls when you were sent to get barbecue sandwiches from the carline cafe across from the crawfish pond and some of which were his own) that always used to make me think about the good time places in such patent leather avenue towns as St. Louis, Missouri and Reno, Nevada and San Francisco, California, where he had played when he was on the road.

Then when you heard him vamping into his own very special stop-time version of "I'll See You in My Dreams" you knew he was about to ride out in up-tempo, riffing chorus after chorus while modulating from key to key so smoothly that you hardly noticed until you tried to whistle it like that.

When you were lucky enough to be there when he was playing for himself that was sometimes also your chance to find out from him about some of the ABC's of piano music just as you were now and then able to find out from Gator Gus about pitching, when you were lucky enough to be around when he and Big Earl were off to themselves working out. Which is why so much of what I was to learn about music comes more directly from Stagolee Dupas than from Luzana Cholly, (who was there first but whom I never saw or heard practicing and never heard even mention either a note or a key signature by name). Because he (Stagolee) was the one who was if anything even more concerned with instrumentation than with lyrics (which as often as not he only scatted anyway—even when the words were his own).

But just as the best of all the very good times to see Gator Gus throwing at top form was when he was in a regulation game, so was the Saturday night jook joint function the very best of all legendary times, places and circumstances to listen to Stagolee Dupas strutting his stuff.

That was what Little Buddy Marshall and I were not so much thinking about or even remembering as breathing in anticipation of at the counter in Miss Pauline's Cookshop, where we sat eating fried mullet with hot sauce and bakery bread and drinking Nehi Orange Crush. I was going to share a piece of leadbelly cake with him and he was going to share his Cincinnati cake with me, and then we were going up to Stranahan's Store and go fifty on next week's package of One Elevens (which we liked better than either Camels or Lucky Strikes in those days) and then we were going to make the rounds.

Miss Pauline stood behind the counter looking at us with her arms folded. Everybody gave her credit for running what was absolutely the very cleanest and most respectable cookshop in Gasoline Point, and when people (especially churchfolks) wanted to eat good cookshop cooking in peace and quiet that was where they used to go. Not that even the most circumspect of Amen Corner church members were ever likely to claim that Miss Pauline, as good a cook as she was, turned out meals in the class with those you got when you ate at Miss Armanda Scott Randolph's next to Stranahan's, or at Papa Gumbo Willie's Hole-in-the-Wall, next to the barbershop. But you never knew what you might get caught in the middle of when you went into Miss Armanda Scott Randolph's anytime after the pay whistles blew on Saturday, and The Hole-in-the-Wall was always off limits to minors even though the barbershop was not.

Y'all going to Sabbath School in the morning, Miss Pauline said as Little Buddy Marshall and I knew she would sooner or later.

Yessum, I said, as much as I had come to dread going to church by that time.

If it don't be raining, Little Buddy said.

Lord, sure do look like it just might, y'all, Miss Pauline said.

You think it will, Miss Paul? Little Buddy said wishfully.

Lord's will be done, Lil Son, she said.

I'm Lil Buddy, Miss Paul, Little Buddy said.

Lil Buddy, Miss Pauline said. That's right. Big Buddy's boy.

I sure do hope it don't, Little Buddy said and Miss Pauline thought he was talking about what she was thinking about, but I knew he was all set to go to see Gator Gus pitch against Bayou la Batre.

But y'all musn't let a little rain stop you from your duty to the Lord now.

Nome, I said.

A fair-weather Christian ain't no Christian atall.

Yessum, I said.

Smell like something burning, Miss Paul, Little Buddy said, and she scooted back into the kitchen, and Little Buddy looked at me and hunched up his shoulders and started fingering the counter as if it were a keyboard.

126

You know yeah, I said, thinking about our regular listening place in the fence corner outside Sodawater's, from which you could hear all of the music and the dancing too, but all you could see were the silhouettes by the windows and whatever chanced to happen in the yard.

Miss Pauline came back in and stood looking at us again.

How Miss Melba and them, Scooter?

Just fine, Miss Paul, I said and that was when I told her that Mama and Papa had gone up the Southern to visit Granpa Gipson and wouldn't be coming back until around midnight, and that was all I said because that was all I needed to say. Because I knew exactly what Miss Pauline was going to say as soon as she saw Mama the next time: The little man was around to see me Saddy night, him and Lil Brother Marshall. And that would be that, because Miss Pauline would be so carried away about me coming to visit her because I just liked to come by to see her every now and then (which was true) that Mama wouldn't have the heart to tell her that I was there because that was where I was supposed to stay until bedtime. So naturally she wouldn't ever get around to checking up to find out if I had.

Us know good and well where Big Buddy Marshall at, don't we Lil Son, Miss Pauline said, referring to the fact that Mister Big Buddy Marshall had spent every Saturday night of the last ten months trying to woo Little Buddy's mama back home. Where Lil Sue?

Over to Aun Law.

And big Bro and Missy with they ma?

Yamn, Lil Buddy said.

That was when Miss Pauline came from behind the counter and went to the front door and stood fanning the apron up toward her face with both hands. Outside the twilight sky was somewhat overcast, but not yet threatening. Little Buddy and I went on eating, hoping the weather would hold up at least until midnight. It could rain all it wanted to after that and continue on into the morning to boot so long as it then cleared up and dried off in time for the game with Bayou La Batre.

Listen, I remember hearing Miss Pauline saying suddenly, and we turned and saw her with one foot outside and her head lifted and turned to one side trying to catch something with her ear. Y'all come here and listen.

What in the name of the Lord in Heaven is that now? she said, and we jumped down and ran to where she was.

Lord, what is it? she said again and then we heard it.

Lord have mercy on this land, she said. Because it sounded like an automatic pistol somewhere up in the direction of Tin Top Alley and there was also the sound of people yelling back and forth at each other and then there were four quick automatic sounding bursts again.

Jesus, I just wonder what in the name of the Lord these crazy sinful drunken niggers already done started this Saddy night and it ain't even good dark yet, Miss Pauline began saying.

You couldn't make out where it was or what it was, but the very first thing that popped into my mind was Earl Joe Timberlake, the new Deputy Sheriff for the last six months following the death of Bam Buchanan, his notorious predecessor, whose car had spun out of control while he was chasing a bootlegger, (probably either Shorty Red or Cholly Chastang) out on the Citronelle Road. Because the very first thing he was reported to have announced as soon as they pinned the star on him was that he was going to ride herd on Gasoline Point niggers until times got tolerable on Saturday nights.

Sound like it might be somewhere up around Tin Top, Little Buddy said sucking his teeth.

I was still thinking about Earl Joe Timberlake.

Hey, Little Buddy said, you don't reckon that's old Earl Joe out here already do you?

Lord I pray, Miss Pauline said. Crackers and niggers. Lord I pray. Crackers and niggers on Saddy night.

Aw shoot, Little Buddy said before I could get the words out myself. Man you know what that is. Man, we supposed to known what that is from the very first off.

Well for God's sakes what in the name of the Lord is it, Lil Bubber?

It's just somebody in a car, Miss Paul, I said then.

Lord, boy what kind of car is that, now?

It's a Hudson Super-Six, Little Buddy told her. But not Mister Long George.

They got it fixed so they can make it backfire like that, I put in.

What on earth for, Lil Man, she said to me.

They just out having them some fun.

Fun? Lord have mercy on some of these old niggers always doing some old crazy foolishness like that now and talking about they having fun. Boy, what kind of fun is that? Lord, I get so sick and tired of these niggers they won't serve God and aint going to make nothing out they life on earth neither.

Little Buddy and I were listening outside again then and there was no question but that it was an automobile because you could also hear the cut-out roaring closer and closer. And then there were three more pops, and the roar faded on away along US 90 and across Cochrane Bridge and into the canebrakes of Baldwin County.

Man, I don't know who that is, Little Buddy said.

Lord deliver us from niggers like that, don't care who it is, Miss Pauline said. Lil Man, you and Lil Son better not never let me catch neither one of y'all out somewhere cutting up and carrying on like that. Just do what you going to do and go about your business. You don't have to be going around trying to wake up creation just to let somebody know you coming somewhere.

Still grumbling under her breath, she started fanning herself with the apron again. Then as she turned to go back into the kitchen we put the money on the counter.

Be seeing you soon, Miss Paul, I said.

Me too, Little Buddy said. Real soon, Miss Paul.

God bless you honeypie, and y'all stay out of devilment.

And that was also when she said what she said about trouble being the one thing you were always sure to find anytime you went looking for it. (By devilment she meant the kind of mischief she assumed boys like me and Little Buddy were forever initiating.)

Outside we came on through Gins Alley by Miss Blue Eula Bacote's flower yard. It was still twilight but now you could see the headlights coming and going along Buckshaw, and then that was where we were, and you could see all the way up to the light on the sign in front of Stranahan's.

Then we were in and out of there with the cigarettes without arousing anybody's suspicions, and at last it was completely dark. But this time instead of heading for the church supper where the girls were we went on along past the Tin Top Alley corner and on up the red clay hill by African Hill Baptist Church to the Southern Overpass just having a good time walking and smoking and talking with the best part of Saturday night still to come.

But we were where we were and saw as much as we saw of what happened between Stagolee Dupas and Earl Joe Timberlake that Saturday night because when, after all that waiting, it was finally time to head for Sodawater's, Little Buddy said what he said about circling by Joe Lockett's-in-the-Bottom to listen to Claiborne Williams for a little while, since we were already that close to that part of town.

Which just goes to show how things sometimes turn out. Because not only was Joe Lockett's-in-the-Bottom where everybody, including Stagolee himself was that night, but even if what happened had happened at Sodawater's all we would have been able to see would have been people running and scattering in the darkness. Because we would not have been spying from any tree at all, not to mention one as close and branches as thick as that. It was even better than a seat in the grandstand.

Because from up where we were looking and listening that night you could see right down through the wide open double windows to the piano and part of the dance floor. I think Joe Lockett was still using gasoline compression lamps in those days (when electricity was still something very special) but the light near the piano was bright enough for you to see them dancing and see Claiborne Williams at the keyboard with his hat cocked to left and his wide silk four-in-hand tie flipped back over his right shoulder, spanking and tickling his kind of blues. I can still remember the kind of hand tailored high-waist sharkskin pants he always used to wear and how his suspenders and arm garters always used to match because they also were made to order; and something else he always wore when he was dressed up was shirts with French cuffs because he was the one who didn't wear rings but used to like to flash the fanciest cuff links you ever saw.

Then we looked and saw that Stagolee himself was also there. He was on the other side of the dance floor (standing with his left leg dropped back and his right foot forward and turned in and his left shoulder lower than his right) laughing and talking with a circle of women around him.

Tonight he was wearing a sporty gray checked pinchback suit, a black silk shirt open at the collar, and a black and gray hound's tooth cap, with the visor unsnapped. All he ever drank during the daylight hours was black coffee, but now he was holding the fruit jar of whiskey that he called his percolating juice, and every now and then one woman would take it and help herself to a sip and then hand it back and give him a kiss on the cheek.

We could hardly believe our luck. The whole house was rocking solid already, and you knew the music was going to keep on getting better and better, not only because Claiborne Williams had not even really warmed up yet, but mainly because, as anybody could see, he was playing as much for Stagolee and himself as for the dancers. Not that he was trying to show off in front of him. Not Claiborne Williams. Because he was too much of an expert in his own right to have to try to impress anybody. Or to have to try to challenge anybody either. Not him. All he was doing was acknowledging that the Stagolee Kid, who was somebody to be recognized, was there and was welcome. Because not only did the two of them like each other too much to challenge each other in front of anybody else, they also enjoyed listening to each other too much ever to do anything except play leapfrog with each other: It was almost as if Claiborne Williams was the pastor making a visiting preacher feel at home by making sure that the congregation was worked up to the right pitch of receptivity before turning over the pulpit to him.

All of which, so far as Little Buddy Marshall and I were concerned, made for the very best of all possible situations. Because a knock-down-drag-out contest between them would have been something to witness all right. No doubt about that. But I for one still don't believe that any music they might have made while frankly trying to outdo each other would have been as good as what you always heard when they used to play as if they were members of the same band. And besides, although by that time we had come to think almost as much of Stagolee as we did of Luzana Cholly (who absolutely could do no wrong) we also liked Claiborne Williams too much to want to take sides against him.

You could see and feel by the way the two of them kept nodding and winking back and forth at each other how much fun they were already having. Then when Claiborne Williams was satisfied that the time was right. he played one more low down bumpy grind and began doodling the introduction to one of his shakehouse shouts and that was when Stagolee moved over to where the piano was and put his fruit jar on top of it and stood clapping his hands and snapping his fingers with the women around him doing the shimmieshewobble and the messaround.

That was when Claiborne Williams started talking down to his fingers and the keyboard saying Hey to his right hand, Well all right to his left, and Yeah mama yeah big mama yeah pretty mama to the piano. Saying: Get away skinny papa to his right hand skipping city. Then saying: Strut to me big mama to his left as it walked the dog. Just bring your big old fine big butt self right on here to me big mama. Now listen to skinny papa. Now what you say big mama. You tell em big mama. I hear you big mama.

Bring it to me. Bring it to me. Bring it to me big mama, he said, and then he let his right hand do the talking and his left hand do the walking until the break which Little Buddy Marshall and I could tell was the last break before the outchorus, and that was when he finally shouted: Watch out here I'm coming. Here I'm coming. Here I'm coming. GodDAMN here I'm coming. As we also knew he would.

That was all for him for the time being then, and he stood up bowing and mopping his face, shifting the handkerchief from one hand to the other as he held out his right and then his left arm for the two women helping him to get his coat back on. Then he straightened his tie and turned up his lapels to protect his chest against cooling off too fast, and then he took a sip from the flask one of the women handed him.

You couldn't hear what he and Stagolee were saying, because the whole place was still in such an uproar. But you didn't need to, because all you had to do was look at them and you could see that they were saying what they always said at a time like that: Man you got it. Man you got it and gone. Man not me. Man you the one. Man me I'm just scuffling trying to make me a little meat and bread to stay alive. Man you was mean up there just now. You was cruel man. You didn't show me no mercy at all man. Man I might as well turn around and go back where I come from. Y'all hear this lying dog. Stagolee Dupas you ought to be shame of yourself. Nigger cut out this shit and get your near-yaller ass on down on that piano stool before these niggers realize how much time I done taken up from you already. Just don't scandalize me too bad man. Just remember I still got to live with these niggers when you back over yonder. Then Claiborne Williams moved on into the next room probably to get something to eat.

That was when Stagolee took off his coat and laid it across the top of the piano and sat down and flipped his visor up. He took his own good time opening a fresh pack of One Elevens, took out two, lit one and put the other one behind his ear like a pencil. Then he crossed his legs and, only half facing the keyboard, began fiddling and diddling with his right hand with his left hand still in his lap, deliberately cooling the house down at the same time that he was warming himself up.

Watching him you could tell that he really felt like playing by the way he let his hand dance all the way up to the highest notes and then snatched it back and snapped his fingers and then sent them flittering up the scale again; and for all the differences between being there listening to honky-tonk and zonky-donk music and being on the sidelines looking at a baseball game, what you felt was almost exactly the same sense of all but unbearable anticipation you got waiting for Gus the Gator to dig in.

But the warm-up was all we got to hear that night. Because just as I was about to whisper Here we go to Little Buddy, he hissed to me. And I looked and there. was an automobile with a spotlight turning into the front yard, and before you could catch your breath the brakes had grabbed, and the driver had sprung out yelling All right in here you niggers, this is the LAW! All right in here you niggers, let's GO, and people were already stampeding and breaking out through all the windows and hightailing it off in every direction.

Then there was nobody there but Earl Joe Timberlake and Stagolee, plus the two of us who were still outside in the tree because it had all happened so fast that we hadn't had time to get down. Stagolee had stood up and was puting his coat back on not only as if nothing had interrupted him, but also as if Earl Joe Timberlake, standing wide legged in his khaki twill surveyor's breeches and lace-up boots with his star pinned onto his notorious, crisply ironed white broadcloth Van Heusen shirt and his thumbs hooked into his pistol belt, was nobody he had ever even heard of. No wonder you suddenly realized how empty and quiet

135

everything was. And no wonder it was also as if stopping the music had somehow stopped time itself.

I remember the two of them there saying nothing and the two of us outside waiting for time to move again because that would be our chance to get gone. And I will never forget what happened next, because that was the very last thing that either Little Buddy or I could or would have sworn before a Grand Jury that either of us had actually seen or heard: Earl Joe Timberlake with his thumbs still hooked into his pistol belt and his long-blocked, side-rolled sheriff's hat pushed back, walking over and raising his foot to start kicking the keys off the piano, and Stagolee saying I wouldn't do that if I was you, whitefolks, and Earl Joe Timberlake whirling and grabbing for his .38 Special.

All I can remember after that is us running and how I felt when I finally made it inside the chinaberry yard once more. I still can't even say whether we slid back down or jumped down. I can very vaguely remember Little Buddy splitting off and breaking for his house, but mainly because the time between there and the gate was when all there was was the wind in my ears getting louder and louder.

So I didn't hear any shots and neither did Little Buddy Marshall. But late that Saturday morning Earl Joe Timberlake's body was found slumped forward over the steering wheel of his Straight Eight on the other side of town about seventeen miles out on the Chunchula Road with one bullet in his hip and one through his head. And Monday there was a picture of him on the front page of the *Mobile Register* and the news story beneath reported that the circumstances surrounding the murder or perhaps more precisely the assassination of Deputy Sheriff Earl Joseph Brantley Timberlake could only be described as mysterious to say the least what with so much conflicting detail, but that all-told the strongest evidence seemed to indicate that the crime had been perpetrated by one ring of bootleggers who had gone to some lengths to leave investigating authorities the impression that the deed was the work of a rival ring.

And later on there was also some very frank speculation about whether Deputy Timberlake himself had not had ties with one or even several bootleg rings, not all of them local and at least one with a direct pipeline to Cuba. And there are also those who still believe that it all had some connection with the death of Bam Buchanan, which very few ever really believed had been due to an automobile accident anyway.

But as little as we actually saw before we hit the wind, Little Buddy Marshall and I could have solved the so-called mystery with one word: *Suicide.* Because that was exactly what we had seen Earl Joe Timberlake about to commit. Because as bad as he not only went for but in fact was, he still was not that bad, for all the good times he had broken up already that year, and for all that kicking the keys off honky-tonk pianos was already known to be one of his special trademarks.

Man you know what I say, Little Buddy said that next Monday afternoon. Man I say shame on him. Man I say he met his mammy-hunching granny-dodging daddy drunk and no better for him. And then he said: Hey I wouldn't do that if I was you Mister Goddamn Peckerwood Motherfucker. And that was when I said: When you come in here kicking on that piano, Mister Sommiching Whitefolks you kicking on me.

Then Little Buddy said: Hey you what the very last thing that supposed to be so mean-ass peckerwood saw in this life. Them piano keys giving him a great big old pearly grin from ear to ear. And I said: Man you know what I keep thinking about? That wasn't even old Stagolee's own piano. Man, I bet you anything old Stagolee ain't never owned his own piano in his life.

Deljean McCray, who was as cinnamon-bark brown as was the cinnamon-brown bark she was forever chewing and smelling like, and who is always the girl I remember when I remember dog fennels and dog fennel meadows, was that much older and that much taller than I was at that time, and she was also two grades ahead of me in school then. So when she finally said what I had been waiting and wishing all day for her to say about me that Wednesday while Miss Tee was downtown shopping, I crossed my fingers.

Then I said what I said. I said Cute is what some folks say about monkeys and puppies, and I held my breath and waited for her to say That's all right about some old monkeys and puppies, ain't nobody talking about no monkeys and puppies I'm talking about you, and she did and poked out her mouth, and she was also trying to roll her eyes. But she couldn't look scornful because she couldn't keep her eyes from twinkling at the same time. Then she started grinning to herself but as if for both of us.

So I said What's so funny girl, but only to be saying something. Because I knew we were thinking about the same thing, which was that Miss Tee, who was the only one who knew we were there by ourselves, was not due back until half-past three. Mama knew where I was (as she usually did, or so she thought) and she knew who else was there because everybody knew where Deljean McCray, who was Miss Tee's husband's niece, was staying that year. But nobody knew that Miss Tee herself was not only not there but was all the way downtown at Askins Marine. Except us. To whom, by the way, her only word had been: If anybody come tell them I say I'll be back directly.

You, Deljean McCray said still pretending to pout, that's what. And I held my fingers crossed but I could hardly keep myself from grinning for another reason.

Because I was thinking about Little Buddy and old Gander Gallagher who were shrimping and crabbing together somewhere near or under One Mile Bridge that day and who thought I was not supposed to go anywhere beyond the chinaberry yard because I was being punished—and who could not possibly know that I was only now on the verge of getting my very first chance to do what they had never let me deny I had been doing all along.

We were in that part of the house because that was where we had brought the clothesbasket, and she was standing at the long table because that was where she was separating what she was supposed to press from all the starched shirts and dresses that had to be sprinkled to be ironed by Miss Tee herself. I was sitting straddling the turned-around cane-bottom chair by the window, and outside there was the castor bean plant. Then there was the chicken yard, and beyond that was the empty clothesline; and you could also see across the garden fence and pass the live oak tree to the meadow and the tank yard.

I kept my fingers crossed because that was the way I already was about almost everything even then. Because by that time I knew better than to take anything for granted even when it was something you had not only been promised but had also been reassured about. The best way was to wait and see, as you had long since learned to do at santaclaustime and for birthday presents. Anyway I was not about to make any country breaks that day. Not with Deljean McCray.

She said she bet me that was what I did like, and I said I bet I didn't either, and she said I bet you do too. I bet you that's exactly what you do like, a puppy dog a littleold hassle mouth frisky tail daddy fyce puppy dog. And she kept on grinning her cinnamon bark grin to herself looking at me sideways. So I frowned and looked out through the window and across the dog fennel meadow to the pine ridge sky above Chickasabogue Creek and Hog Bayou Swamp, but I was almost grinning to myself in spite of myself then because she was the one who had said it first. So all I said was How come you say that, and she said Because, and I said Because what, girl, and she said don't be calling her no girl.

Little old mister boy, she said.

Well, miss girl then, I said. Because what miss girl?

Because you don't even know what I'm talking about, that's what, she said, and I said That's what you say.

Because I did know. Because I already knew about all of that even before that time playing house with Charlene Wingate when I was not only caught and not only spanked and chastised but also threatened with the booger man who would catch you and cut off your thing with his butcher knife.

That's what you say, I said, but that don't make it so, and that was when she said Well I bet you, and I said Bet me what, and she said You guess what since you know so much about it, and I said okay, and I almost uncrossed my fingers. But I didn't. Beacuse I could hardly wait, but I knew I had to. So all I did was get up from the chair with my fingers crossed in my left pocket.

I was standing that close to her and the Vaseline sheen of her cinnamon scented braids then, and she said: You know something you a mannish little old boy, Scooter. You just as mannish as you can be. Boy, who you call yourself getting mannish with? Boy, what you think you trying to do? Boy you better let your pants alone. Boy, who told you to come trying to start something like that? Ohh Scooter.

She moved back to the wall then and said Ohh Scooter look at you. Look at yours. Look at you already swelling up like that. Did a wasp sting you or something. Oh Scooter you mannish rascal you. But see there you ain't got no hairs like me yet. Just like I thought. See there. Look at me.

Look at my titties like a big girl, she said, smelling almost as much like sardines as cinnamon. Look at my hairs like a wasp nest. And she bent her knees with her back against the wall and put her hands inside her thighs around her dog fennel meadow and her sardine slit. See there. I'm already a big girl little old mannish boy. I'm already big enough to get knocked up. Because a girl grown enough to have a baby just as soon as she old enough to start ministrating. If I was to do it with a sure enough man and he was to shoot off and big me he got to marry me unless he want to go to jail.

That was also when she said what she also said about boys being different. Boys can get stunted: Little old mannish tail boys start messing around with too many big girls and grown women before you man enough and you know what? You subject to hurt yourself and come up stunted for the rest of your life. That's what they say happened to Billy Goat. They say somebody got a hold to him and turned every way but loose and now his thing too big for the rest of his body, and that's how come he have them falling out spells gagging and foaming at the mouth. Some old hard woman bring your nature down too soon and that's when it go to your head and you start craving and playing with yourself and skeeting all the time and goodbye, sonny boy.

That's all right about Goat Bascomb, I said thinking also of Knot Newberry the hunchback who went around whispering and giggling to himself. That's Goat. That ain't got nothing to do with me.

Because if I was going to be stunted I would have already been stunted a long time ago, I said and she said: Who you think you trying to fool, Scooter? Who you think this is you talking to? Who you trying to say you been doing something like that with little old mannish pisstail boy?

Girl you know good and well ain't nobody supposed to tell you who nobody was, I said.

And I bet you I know why too, she said. Because it ain't nobody that's why. Because I sure know one thing. It wasn't nobody big as me. And little old pisstail gals don't count. Because I bet you I already know who it was anyhow. Because it ain't nobody but little old Charlene Wingate with her little old half stuck-up frizzly-headed self, and she sure don't count because she ain't got no more than some little old pimples on her little flat bosom and I bet you anything she ain't got no hairs yet.

That's all right about who it was, I said and I was also about to say that's all right about big girls and grown

women and all that too, but that was when I realized that
she was standing there grinning at me sideways because she
was probably waiting for me to be the one to make the next
move. So I said something else.

You said you bet me Deljean, I said. You the one said
you bet me.

Well come on then little old mannish boy, she said.
Since you think you already such a mister big man. What
you standing there sticking out like that for?

That was that first time with Deljean McCray (on the
floor under the tent top of the table with my fingers crossed
all the while) and she kept saying What you doing boy?
Boy what you think you doing you little fresh tail rascal.
Boy, Scooter I declare. Boy, Scooter here you doing something like this. Oh see there what you doing? Now sure
enough now Scooter now boy now you know good and well
we not supposed to be doing nothing like this.

Then she said Now that's enough now Scooter so you
stop now and I mean it too now Scooter. Get up off of me
boy. You get your fresh-ass self down off me. Then we were
standing up again and she said Oh Scooter what you been
doing? Boy what you think you been doing? Now you going
somewhere talking about you been doing that with a big
girl now ain't you? Now tell the truth. Because that's all
right with me. Because you better not tell nobody who it
was just like you wouldn't tell me on little old skinny butt
Charlene Wingate.

144

Boy Scooter, she said not only pointing but aiming her finger at me with one eye closed, Boy if you tell somebody on me boy you sure going to wish you hadn't when I get through with you. Boy you go somewhere and tell somebody something like this on me and I will natural born fix you sonny boy and I mean it Scooter and if you don't believe it just go on somewhere and say something and see. Because you know what I'm going to do I'm going to say you didn't do nothing but come up there acting just like some little old daddy fyce puppy dog and all I did was start to laughing and laughed you right on out of here. I declare I will. I declare before God I will Scooter.

But then she was also grinning as if for both of us again, and she pushed me and said: I just said that. You know I just said that don't you Scooter? You know I just said that just to see because you already know you all right with me don't you Scooter?

The next time was that day coming through Skin Game Jungle on the way back from taking the twelve o'clock basket to Mr. Paul Miles at Blue Rock mill when she said Hey wait a minute Scooter because I got to squat. Hey ain't you got to do something too? Hey I bet you something. Hey you know what I bet you? I bet you you still ain't got nothing down there but your thing. I bet you you ain't even starting in to sprout your first fuzz yet. Now tell the truth now Scooter. That's how come you shamed to pee now ain't it?

She said That's all right about your thing. Ain't nobody talking about that. I'm talking about some hairs. I'm talking about what I'm doing doing something like that with some little old boy ain't even old enough to do nothing but some dog water. Because when you first start to have to shave with a sure enough razor and lather that's how you know when a boy already getting to be a man enough to make a baby. That's what I'm talking about. I'm talking about some sure enough doing it like some sure enough grown folks with your hair mingling together and all that and then the man shoot off. That's what I'm talking about.

But that was also the time when she said: What you standing there holding yourself looking at me like that for. Come on boy because that's all right about that just this one more time.

❁

The time after that, which was that day while Mama and Miss Tee were up in Chickasaw with Miss Liza Jefferson, was my first time in a real bed with no clothes on, and she said I'm going to show you something this time, and she did. She said I bet you you don't even know what that is. That's just the old Georgia grind, and this the gritty grind. I bet you you ain't never done the sporty grind before. She said This the bobo and this the sporty bobo and this the whip and this the bullwhip and this the snatch. She said When the man put his legs like that with his arms like that he straddling the mountain and the woman can do the greasy pole and when the woman put up her self like this that mean the man can come to the buck and when me and you go like this that's what you call bumping the stump.

She said When you see me doing this that's when I'm doing my belly roll to sell my jelly roll. Like Miss Sweetmeat Thompson. Like Miss Big Money Watkins. Then she said What you going do when I sic my puppies on you like Miss Slick McGinnis all the way out in San Fransisco? and I said Sic them back that's all right who like. Because I couldn't make up my mind whether I wanted to be like Stagolee or Luzana Cholly or Elmore Sanders. And that's when she said Well let me see you sic them then and started snapping her fingers and sucking her breath through her teeth.

I don't remember when I uncrossed my fingers that time. All I have ever been able to recollect about what happened next is hearing her whisper Oh shit oh hell oh goddamn and then saying Oh shit now oh hell now oh goddamn now Scooter. And suddenly I was not sure that I was not about to begin to spurt blood from somewhere in the very center of my being and I didn't even care. Because in that same instant it was as if you were coming through the soft stream-warm velvet gates to the most secret place in the world, and I had to keep on doing what I was doing no matter what happened.

And I did. By reaching and by holding and by floating and by pushing and by slipping and sliding and slittering and by hithering and by thithering through cinnamon scented sardine oil and dog fennel thickets and dog fennel meadows.

Then afterwards she said What did I tell you? Didn't I tell you? Oh Scooter see there? Oh Scooter you little rascal you just now losing your cherry. Scooter boy you done lost your cherry just like I told you. What did I tell you? I told you about messing around with big girls now didn't I? Oh

Scooter you done lost your cherry and I bet you I know who the one took it.

❂

The one who wrote: *Dear SP guess who (smile) you are my SP because you so cute and also sweet from X guess who (smile) XXX is for hug and kisses for smiles (smile)*, was Elva Lois Showers, who was also the one who started saying Please don't now stop that now as soon as I touched her arm. Please don't please don't. Not now Scooter. Now boy you better stop. You better stop that now Scooter.

Please don't what, I said.

You know what, she said You know good and well what. Just behave yourself. Just don't be doing nothing trying to do that. How come you cain't just be nice, Scooter?

That was when we were in the eighth grade and her seat was three rows over and she answered the roll call after *Ross, J. T.* and before *Singleton, Fred Douglass*. So I knew whose handwriting it was as soon as I unfolded the note, because that was also when everybody used to have to go to the blackboard to write sentences almost as often as you used to have to go work problems in arithmetic. I didn't look over that way for the rest of that afternoon, and I could hardly wait for the last bell so I could be all to myself and read it again.

I felt good thinking and whistling about it all the way home, and I went to sleep thinking about it and I woke thinking and whistling about it. But all I did when I got back to school was act as if nothing had happened. So I worried all the way home that next day and spent that night wondering what you were supposed to do, but then the day after that every time I had to stand up to recite I felt that good, warm, feathery-light way you feel when you realize (without having to look) that somebody is looking at you because she has been thinking about you.

Which is why on the way out for twelve o'clock recess I got to the door at the same time as she did and said what I said. I said Hello. (Not only like a big boy but also like a big schoolboy. All I had ever said to her or to any other girl before was Hey. Hey Elva Lois what you know. Hey Elva Lois what you doing. Hey Elva Lois girl where you been. Where you going.) I said Hello and she turned up her nose and ran on out to the girls' play area behind Willie Mae Crawford before I could even say Elva Lois. But that next morning there was another note: S is for secret and P is for passion (smile) F is for how come you try to be so fresh (smile).

So that was the day I carried her books as far as the Hillside Store fork the first time, and all I did was say Bye and came back whistling and the next day there was the next note: *Thinking of somebody very very sweet guess who (smile) XXX kisses (smile)*. But as soon as I did what I did that next time she said what she said and pulled away and ran half way down Martin's Lane before she turned and blew lilac time kisses at me from both hands before going through the gate.

The next time and the time after that and the time after that and so forth she also said and said and said: How come you always got to come getting so fresh with some-body, Scooter? Boy, I'm telling you. That's all you think about. How come you can't just be my SP and be nice? How come every time we get somewhere like this you al-ways got to start acting like that? I'm talking about every time, Scooter. I'm talking about every time. Everytime we somewhere out of sight. Everytime we happen to come by some old empty house or something. Everytime we somewhere and it start to get dark. And don't let it start to raining.

There was also the time when she said: How come you can't just be nice like in class? That's when you so smart and neat and everybody always talking about you so cute, and come to find you just as big a devil as you can be, Scooter. Boy, I'm telling you; you sure got Miss Lexine Metcalf fooled. You and David Lovett. That's all he think about too. Just like you. That's what Clarice say and I sure can believe it now. Scooter y'all think y'all something just because Miss Lexine Metcalf think y'all so smart, don't you? Y'all think somebody supposed to let you do that just because she always talking about you and him the two main boys know your homework so good all the time. Well let me tell you something. Don't nobody care nothing about what no Miss Lexine Metcalf say, Scooter. Because she just makes me so sick carrying on like that about some little old fresh boys like you and little old David Lovett anyhow. Because she ain't doing nothing but giving y'all the big head nohow. Because that's exactly how come y'all think y'all so cute somebody supposed let y'all do something like that any time you want to. Especially you, Scooter. Just because some old Miss Lexine Metcalf talking about you going to amount to something so important some of these days.

If that's the way you feel, I said. If that's how you want to be, Elva Lois.

Now that ain't what I said, Scooter, she said. Ain't nobody said nothing about that. You don't even know what I'm talking about. You might know how to get your lesson but that don't mean you know something about what girls talking about. You don't know nothing about no girls, boy.

Then she promised. And I almost believed her. Because that was when she said: Sure enough now Scooter. But not right now Scooter. Not this time Scooter. I got to go now Scooter. I got to be back home now. Didn't I say I would? I already told you, Scooter. This not fair for you to come trying to do that when I already told you. See that's what I'm talking about. And I already said I would.

But she never did. Because what she said that next time was I promised you and now you supposed to promise me something too. And when I said That's not what you said, she said I don't care what I said that's what I meant, because that's what I always meant. When the girl say yes, you supposed to do what she say first, Scooter.

So that was all that ever became of me and Elva Lois Showers that spring which I also remember because the song that was featured during the baseball games was "Precious Little Thing Called Love." Because I was not about to cut my finger and swear by my blood. Not me. I said I don't care Ela Lois. I said That's all right with me because I don't care.

Shoot goddamn right, Little Buddy said when I told him about it that same night. Shoot man what she think this is. Shoot Elva Lois Showers. Shooot she all right but she ain't all that pretty. Shooot tell her she crazy, man. Shoot tell her that's what the goddamn hell SP suppose to mean, some you know what. Secret just meant on the QT. Shoot tell her if she won't, somegoddamnbody else sure will. Elva Lois Showers. Shoot. Man I just can't get over that heifer. Elva Lois Showers. Goddamn. Shoot.

One somebody else who always would be on the QT was Beulah Chaney (who should have been at least two grades ahead of me at that time but whose seat was by the window in the first row behind Walter Lee Cauldwell). She was the one who said I got something for you, Scooter, that day at the blackboard while everybody else was outside for Maypole practice.

I ain't going tell you what because if you don't already know that's just too bad. If somebody got to tell you that, all I can say you not old enough yet. So if you want me to give it to you you got to come where I say when I say.

She lived at the edge of Chickasabogue Bottom. To get there you had to go along the AT & N toward Chickasaw until you came to Blue Poplar Crossing. Then you cut through that part of Parker's Mill Quarters to the elderberry corner and came all the way down the three-quarter mile winding slope, and you could see the barn and the wood-shed under the moss draped trees beyond the open wagon gate.

Well I declare Scooter, she said that first time, Here you all the way over here sure enough. Boy what if I just said that just to see? What if I just said that just to see if I could fool you to come way over here?

But she had not. She was surprised but anybody could see how pleased she also was, and before I could stop grinning long enough to put on my frown and say Oh Beulah Chaney, she said Come on Scooter. I'm just teasing. You know I'm just teasing you, don't you Scooter? That mean I must like you Scooter. Because when you like somebody, look like you just have to be teasing them and all of that just because you might be kinda glad to see them or something.

But later on in the plum thickets beyond the collard patch (with everybody away because it was Saturday afternoon) she was only half teasing: Oh Scooter I'm surprised at you. I'm talking about you just as sneaky as you can be. How you know this what I was talking about? I coulda been talking about a lost ball I found or something like a mitt or something like that. I coulda been talking about some books and things I found in the bottom of the trunk or something and here you come with this the first thing on your mind just like everybody else just because I said that. You ought to be shamed of yourself Scooter. Now tell the truth ain't you shamed of yourself all the way over here doing something like this?

As if you didn't already know what would start if anybody even so much as suspected that you had ever been there: Hey Scooter where Beulah Chaney? Hey Scooter Beulah Chaney looking for you, man. Hey Scooter Beulah Chaney say come there, man. Hey Scooter Beulah Chaney say she sure do miss you since that last time you come down in the bottom. She say hurry up back. Hey Scooter guess who they say your girl now? Old Beulah Chaney. Hey Scooter here come your new girl!. Old big bottom beulah chaney old pillow busom beulah chaney loping like a milk cow. Hey Scooter you know what she say? She say she got something for you. She say she got some more for you man.

Not that you didn't know there was another side to it all. Because even as they said what they had said to try to scandalize me in front of everybody in the schoolyard during ten o'clock recess that time you could tell that something else was bothering them. And sooner or later somebody was going to bring it up in one way or another (especially somebody two or three grades ahead of you): Hey what some little old scooter butt booty butt squirt like you doing hanging around some old big ass tough ass heifer like Beulah Chaney for? Boy you know what they tell me? They say you over there trying to mind that old funky pussy. They say you ain't nothing but some little old granny-dodging cock knocker, Scooter. So whyn't you just look out the goddamn way, junior? Look out the way and let somebody over in there know how to handle that stuff. Hey you want somebody to show you how to handle some big old heifer like that? Well don't be looking at me because somebody might find out.

Me myself I don't care, she said. Because you think I don't know what they always trying to say about somebody? You think I don't know they always behind somebody's back trying to make some kind of old fun of somebody and calling somebody all them old names. You think don't nobody know what they doing every time they come running up in my face saying something just to see what I'm going to say they can go back somewhere and laugh some more? They think somebody so dumb. They the one dumb.

You the one got everybody fooled. You the one always going around like you so nice you don't never think about nothing like this because you ain't never got no time for nothing but studying something in some of them old books for Miss Lexine Metcalf and here you over here just as soon as I told you something like that.

Calling somebody riney, she said another time, I ain't no riney and they know it. I might be this color, but that don't make nobody no riney. Because look at my hair and look at somebody like old nappy headed Jessie Mae Blount. Ain't nothing on me that red and nappy, and she even got all them freckles and splotches, and ain't nobody never been going around calling her nothing like that. So that's all right with me if they got to say something. Because I don't care. But anytime they come trying to make out like they cain't stand to be getting next to me without turning up their nose and that kind of stuff, that ain't fair. Because

154

some of them might got a few pretty clothes but that don't mean cain't nobody else be just as neat and clean.

She was more yaller than riney and her hair was more of a curly brown than a kinky red and her eyes were blue-green. So what with her living that close to Chickasabogue Swamp and what with her gray-eyed father being a raft man and a boom man who also had a whiskey still somewhere up in Hog Bayou and what with her tallow faced mother (on those rare times you glimpsed her) almost always wearing a bonnet and an apron like somebody from Citronelle or Chastang, Little Buddy and I always took it for granted that she was probably more Cajun than anything else.

What she mostly smelled like was green moss. But that first time it was willow branches then fig branches then plum leaves. Sometimes it was sweetgum leaves plus sweetgum sap. And sometimes it was green pine needles plus pine trunk bark plus turpentine-box rosin. But mainly it was live oak twigs which she chewed plus Spanish moss which she used to make a ground pallet.

She said: Anybody say I ain't just as clean as the next one just plain telling a big old something-ain't-so. Anybody come talking like I might got something somebody subject to be catching from me they just trying to start something about somebody. Like cain't nobody get them back if I want to. You just let them keep on and see. Somebody always trying to think they so much better than somebody. They ain't no better than nobody else. If they think somebody think they better than somebody they must be crazy. Because don't think don't nobody know nothing on every last one of them.

On the other hand there was also Johnnie Mae Lewis with her johnnie mae lewis long legs and her johnnie mae neat waist and her johnnie mae knee stockings and her johnnie mae prompt princess tapered A-plus recitation fingers and her johnnie mae perfect pensmanship who not only said Not me not you Scooter in front of everybody standing by the punch bowl table that afterschool partytime and not only refused my hand before I could get it up but then danced off with Sonny Kemble of all the knuckleheads that I had always thought she wouldn't even speak to and to "Little White Lies" of all the rain sad honeysuckle melodies that I was forever whistling when I was alone with my boy-blue expections and my steel-blue determination that spring the year before Beulah Chaney.

Nor have I forgotten Maecile Cheatham and her chocolate brown dimples and her glossy creek indian black pocahontas braids, who tricked me into saying what I said so she could go back and tell Claribel Owens who said You think you so slick don't you Scooter you go to be so smart and don't even know better than to try to do something like that with somebody's best friend and I'm talking about the very one that already said that's all you trying to see if you can do. I'm talking about the very one already told me about you and Ardelle Foster and you and Julia Glover and you and Evelyn Childs too Mister think you so much and ain't shit Scooter so good bye.

Then that time which is also the baseball spring and summer I remember whenever no matter wherever I hear downhome trombones tailgating "At Sundown" there was also Olivet Dixon with her big bold olivet dixon eyes and her big bold olivet dixon legs and hips and her underslung olivet rubber doll dixon walk that made her seem two or even three years older than I was instead of one year younger. She was the one who said: The one I like is Melvin

Porter because he don't have to always be trying to be some little teacher's pet. Melvin Porter is a real sport. Melvin Porter dress like a real sheik. Melvin Porter is the one all the girls like because he got experience.

melvin porter
melvin porter
melvin porter
melvin porter

He got it and gone all over you any day Scooter. He got experience over you Scooter.

So I said Well good for melvin porter okay for melvin porter hooray for melvin porter melvin porter melvin porter who was the mean sixteen I was still that far away from. Who got her in the family way and hopped a sundown freight train for Los Angeles, California and left her to John Wesley Griffin who was seventeen and who quit school and married her and went to work at Shypes Planer Mill and then lost her to Wendell Robinson who was twenty and was a bellboy downtown at the Battle House and took her to dances on Davis Avenue and got her that way again and went to Chicago and did not send back for her.

❁

The one I remember when I remember crape myrtle yard blossoms is Charlene Wingate, to whom I said what I said when she said You suppose to say roses red and violets blue and you suppose to tell me Charlene I love you and you suppose to ask me Charlene be my valentine and you suppose to call me baby and you suppose to say I'm your sugar and when you say you my sweet one and only you suppose to cross your heart Scooter because when you tell somebody something like that that's when you suppose to promise.

I do Charlene, I said.

And she said I'm talking about sure enough now Scooter because I'm talking about when somebody want somebody to be sweethearts.

And I said Me too Charlene.

And she said Well then.

And I looked at her and her Creole frizzy hair and her honey brown face and her crape myrtle blossom smile and waited.

And she said All you said was you do Scooter do what Scooter you suppose to say it Scooter that's the way you suppose to do.

And that was the very first time I ever said that in my life and that was when she said Well you know what the boy suppose to do when the girl say here I stand on two little chips. And I said Come and kiss your two sweet lips. And that is what I did without even thinking about it. And that was when she said You suppose to whisper darling and you suppose to whisper honey because now we suppose to be sweethearts Scooter.

Which was also when she said When you sweethearts that's when you have sweet heartaches every time you just think about somebody and every time you just hear somebody say that name you have to hold yourself to keep somebody from seeing you looking and when you know you going to be somewhere at the same time you cain't hardly wait and when you see somebody coming and it look like the one you want it to be you have to catch your breath because that's your weakness.

Then when she said How you miss me Scooter how

much you think about me, I said A whole lot Charlene. But I never did what Little Buddy Marshall used to do when he was thinking about Estelle Saunders. Because not only did he used to say Yes sir that's my baby you know don't mean maybe, but sometimes he also used to limp-walk straddling his right hand while swinging his left arm scat singing Has she got da, de da yes she has got dadeda that certain that certain body do she like do de do yes she like my dodedo that certain body of mine.

What I said that first time in the crape myrtle play-house was If we suppose to be playing house we suppose to you know Charlene, and she said First you suppose to go to work Scooter and then I'm suppose to bring you your dinner basket and then you suppose to come home and eat supper and then we suppose to sit in the parlor and then you suppose to stand up and stretch because you ready to go to bed. And then Scooter. That's when Scooter.

The Gins Alley victrola music I remember when I remember Deljean McCray all dressed up and on her way somewhere walking like Creola Calloway and like Miss Slick McGinnis as Little Buddy Marshall and I myself used to walk like Luzana Cholly and also like Stagolee Dupas is Jelly Roll Morton and the Red Hot Peppers playing "Kansas City Stomp" as if in the pre-game grandstand with the pre-game pennants flying and the vendors hawking pre-game peanuts, popcorn, ice cream, candy, hot dogs and barbecue sandwiches, and the circus elephant tuba carrying all the way out to the dog fennels beyond the outfield.

But the song I remember when I remember her snapping her fingers and rolling her stomach and snatching her hips and pouting her lips and winking and rolling her eyes at the same time is "How Come You Do Me Like You Do." And she also used to like to sing "Ja-Da" and You got to hmmm sweet mama or you won't see mama at all. As if she never even heard of the Deljean McCray who was as concerned as it turned out she always was about Miss Tee. About whom she was also the one who said Boy Scooter if she ever find out about me being the one been doing something like this with you every time her back turn boy I just know she subject to just about kill me Scooter. Boy I rather for Miss Melba to be the one any day. And I'm talking about Miss Tee so nice I don't believe she even want to kill a flea. But boy Scooter I just know that woman subject to beat my ass till my nose bleed if she ever find out about me spoiling you like this. Because evrybody know how much she like children especially little old frisky tail boys think they so smart. Because you know what folks say? They say she had her heart set on being a schoolteacher like Miss Lexine Metcalf and Miss Kell and Miss Norris and them. That's how come she got all them books and pretty things and all them flowers and keep her house painted and her fence whitewashed like that. Because all that come from way back when she used to be off in training before she come down here on a visit and ended up getting married to my uncle Paul Boykin. So that's how that happened. Because Uncle Paul said that was that about all of that. So that's when she had to give up on it. And then come to find out they don't look like they going to even get no children of her own for her to bring up with all the schooling she still got.

That's how come she so crazy about children, she also said. And that's how come children so crazy about her.

Because she just like a good teacher because that's the way she talk and she can tell you all about different things and show them all them different games and you don't have to be sitting up in no classroom scared somebody just up there waiting for you to make a mistake or something. Like that Miss booty butt Kell with her booty butt self.

But boy Scooter you the favorite one she like over all of us around here and I'm suppose to be in the family. And I bet you I know how come. You know how come? You want me to tell you how come you the one her natural born pet and don't care who knows it. Them books. Because you the one take to them books like that's your birthmark or something Scooter. And that's what she like better than anything in this world and here you come just as smart as you devilish. And you know it too son. And don't tell me you don't know you her heart. Ain't nothing she got too good for you and you know it. And you know something else I bet you if Miss Melba and Unka Whit let her she would flat out adopt you boy. Everybody know that. Boy Scooter she give anything to get her hands on you for her own. That's how come I just know she'll cold kill me if she ever was to find out about something like this. Because you know she bound to put it all on me just like you didn't have nothing in the world to do with it.

When I came back for Christmas that time and saw her working behind the counter when I went into Smallwoods Cleaning and Pressing Club she said Mister College Boy. Well all right Mister College Boy. Well go on Mister

College Boy. Well excuse me Mister College Boy and I
said Come on Deljean. I said How you been Deljean. I
said I been thinking about you Deljean. I been wondering
what you doing. And she said You the one Scooter. She
said You the one better go on out of here. Boy you know
good and well you not up there with all them high class
college girls thinking about somebody like me. Boy,
Scooter, used to be little old Scooter, tell the truth now,
you forgot all about me up there now didn't you? Boy you
ain't thought about me until just you walked in here and
seen me just now. And I said That's what you say Deljean.
That's what you say.

I said How could somebody ever forget you Deljean.
I said you know something? I don't even have to think
about you Deljean to remember you. Just like I don't have
to think of Little Buddy and Luzana Cholly and Stagolee
and Gator Gus and all that. Because that's the way you
really remember somebody. I said You the one got my
cherry Deljean. I said You remember that time. I said You
the one taught me what it's made for Deljean. I said You
the one used to keep me out of a whole lot of trouble Deljean.

I said Ain't no telling what kind of mess I mighta got
all tangled up in if it hadn't been for you Deljean. And she
said Boy Scooter boy you a lying dog. That ain't the way
I heard it. Boy who you think you coming in here trying to
fool. Because I know exactly who that was from the tenth
grade on. You think don't nobody know about you and her.
And right under Miss Tee's nose and she so glad you
making all them good marks and winning all them scholar-
ship prizes and stuff up there in high school she ain't even
suspected it to this day. But see me myself I know you
Scooter. I mighta been married and having that baby for
that old no good nigger but I bet you I can tell you just

about everything you call yourself doing in them days. I bet you. I even know about you and old big butt Beulah Chaney, Scooter, and I know you didn't know nobody know about that. Because you know what? As soon as I seen you coming out from down over in there one time and I said to myself old Scooter think he so slick but he cain't fool me. Because I know you Scooter, at least I used to know you. Because I don't know nothing about no college boys.

But she also said: Boy Scooter if you ain't still a mess. Here we doing this again. And she said Boy I'm surprised at you Scooter. You suppose to be a college boy. I thought college boys suppose to be so proper. I thought college boys suppose to be so dictified. I thought college boys suppose to be such a gentleman all the time.

That was that next evening. And she also said Well all right Mister College Boy. Well go on then. I see you. You think you something don't you. I didn't teach you that. Did she teach you that. You know who I'm talking about. Didn't no high class college girls teach you that. And that was when she said Boy Scooter Miss Tee sure subject to come over here and kill me if she find out her precious Mister College Boy over here putting in time with this old used to be married woman that didn't go no further than the ninth grade. Specially after all she done for me.

She said: Boy Scooter Miss Tee so proud you up there getting all that good education she don't know what to do. That's all she talk about every chance she get. She still just as nice to me as she can be just like she always was. Just like ain't nothing happened. Except keeping Twenty for me so I can work since I made that old no good nigger get his old lazy ass out of here and he finally went on up north somewhere. But you still the one her heart Scooter. And that's the way she want Twenty to be too. Just like you. You seen Twenty over there. That's what they call him.

For Quinty. Because his name Quinten Roosevelt. Quinten
Roosevelt Hopson. He five and Boy if he turn out to like
his books he got him a home with Miss Tee don't care what
happen to me. Boy she cain't hardly wait to send him to
school so he can get on up there and come by Miss Metcalf like you. With your used to be little old go-to-be-so-
slick self. But you was born marked for it Scooter.

The last time with Deljean McCray was that night
after the Mardi Gras parade when I came back during that
war for that special occasion. It was that many years after
college then, and she said Look at me with these three
children now and getting almost big as a house. And look
at you Scooter used to be that little old think-you-so-smart-
and-cute schoolboy I used to could make him blush anytime I want to. And I said You still can Deljean. I said
What you think I'm doing right now. And she said You
something else Scooter. She said You always been something else Scooter and that's how come you always been
all right with me almost as bad as Miss Tee. And that was
when she said That's the only part that make me feel sorry
about all this happening today. Because she not here to see
you come back this time. Because I can just see her looking
at her mister so proud she can hardly stand it. But that's
how come you still all right with me too Scooter. Because
that's something everybody got to give you your credit for.
Because the one thing she didn't never have to worry about
right on up to her dying day was you trying your best to
make somebody out of yourself.

Which is also when she also said: You know something Scooter. Boy you never could fool me. I'm the one fooled you Scooter. You remember that time when I was the one that got your cherry. Well you suppose to be the one so smart and I bet you a fat man you didn't know that's when you got mine too until I just now told you.

Is she your mama's sister? Your papa's sister? Is she your mama's brother's wife? Your papa's brother's wife? Your mama's own auntee? Your papa's own? Maybe she's your mama's cousin. Your papa's cousin. Maybe she your big half sister by your mama or your papa and somebody else, they used to say. And I always said She's my own auntee. That's why I call her Miss Tee. Because she is the one who always has been my main auntee over everybody else in the whole world.

Maybe she your you know goodfairy godmother, man, Little Buddy Marshall said. You know, he said. Because that's what auntees suppose to be anyhow. That's what mine is and that's how come I call her my Big Auntee, he said. Because that's just exactly what they for. And that's where you can always go when you want to ask for something you already know good and damn well ain't nobody at home to buy for you. And that's how come you can always depend on them for something else for Christmas and Easter and your birthday and something special when you stop by there on the first day of school.

That's how come when you don't have them you have to have a godmother, Little Buddy said. And that really mean she your guard-mother, because she the one suppose to help your sure-enough mama watch out over you. And your Big Uncle is the same thing. Because you know who bought me my big league mitt and mask, and you don't even have to guess who going to be the one to get me my first pair of spikes when the time come. Just like you know good and well you going to be getting yours from the same one your A. G. Spalding glove come from.

Man, look at Aunt Callie Callahan, Little Buddy Marshall also said. Man she everybody's Big Auntee, he said. Because that's what she always acting like, he said.

And I said Callie the Cat. And he put his hands on his hips, held his tongue tucked inside his bottom lip like a dip of Garrett's Snuff and said Chomere and jeer Aunt Chat shome sugar and spice and shome of all that nice prettiness you little ugly grand rascal you.

And I did it too, standing as if I were wearing a pair of unlaced man-sized brogan work shoes. I said: You better bwing your little old rubber butt self on here to Aunt Cat before I bop the flying do-do out of you. Little nasty stinking goodlooking good for nothing honey bung dumpling. Little old billy-smelling sugar-coated puppy dog tail. Jeer Aunt Chat shome more of that honey. Trying to be stingy with it already. Don't you be trying to tease me like no jelly bean. And you better not be calling me no Aunt Cat neither. You little mannish pisstail musrat. You ain't old enough to be talking that kind of talk yet. Let me catch you grinning and calling me the Cat and I'm going to wash you mouth out with lye soap. Be plenty of time for you to find out all about that. And you will too, you little devilish-eyed scoundrels. Ain't neither one of y'all fooling me. I seen you pointing them toes and dropping them hips and sloping them shoulders. Don't be thinking you fooling me, I said, still trying to talk holding my tongue like that. No telling what Miss Melba going to do when she find out you rotten to the core under all that sparkle-eyed sweet talk, I said.

Now as for that Lil Buster Marshall, Little Buddy Marshall said, ain't nothing nobody in the world can do about that rapscallion but get the kidnappers and bootleggers to lose him somewhere up in Hog Bayou Swamp somewhere.

Man, what she talking about? I said. Man, that's where we come from. And he said Yeah in a goddamn skiff boat. And I said Yeah and with no overcoat, remembering Stagolee Dupas singing the dirty verses to "Squeeze Me."

Anytime anybody think I cain't take care of myself in the swamp all they got to do is just try me, he said. Then standing wide legged with his hand down there, he said But man one of these goddamn times she going to be hugging and kissing me like that and godddddamn!

Don't make no difference which side of the family they belong to, Little Buddy Marshall also said one time. Because they don't have to be your flesh and blood kinfolks nohow. Because anybody can be your auntee if they want to. Just like anybody can be your cousin if they want to act like it. And the one you like the best like you like Miss Edie Bell Boykin is your Big Auntee. Just like Aun Law my Big Auntee.

Anybody can be anything you want them to be, he said. And I said the same thing. Then I heard what I heard and had to believe that night at Mister Meadows' wake.

At first, they were sitting on the porch in the dark talking about death again, and this time it was like an invisible sheet that shrouded down over you. But sometimes it was also something with a cold, icy grip and a stone embrace and sometimes, ghost that it was, it came tripping quietly and sometimes, being as it was God's business, it struck like lightning just to remind sinners that God was almighty. It could come at any time and place and in any shape and form and fashion and it took young and old, good and bad on that long lonesome journey across the River Jordan whether they were ready or not which was why Jesus was the only one who could make up your dying bed.

Then they were talking again about that great getting

up morning which was Judgment Day; and that was when, as always, somebody started telling about how he found the truth in the light, got converted and was reborn to be saved in Jesus Christ. And from then on until somebody started another song it was like being in church at confession and determination—telling time, with first one and then another recalling how he was stumbling in darkness until he found the way to the Altar of the Lamb, which was the way to everlasting life.

Somebody kept repeating that, one saying it that way and another saying life everlasting and somebody else saying life eternal; and I thought I knew what the next song was going to be. But when it came it was not "Everlasting Arms," but "Get Right With God"; and when I finally fell on off to sleep with my head on Mama's lap they were singing "The Blood Done Sign My Name," which always made me think how Good Hope Baptist Church people looked coming up out of the baptising pen in the Chickasabogue with the sound of the singing and the shouting echoing all the way across the creek to the canebrakes.

But before that they had been talking about Mr. Ike Meadows himself; and Bro Abe Gardner and Old Tyler McIntosh had started reminiscing and had gone all the way back to the time when the three of them were growing up together back in the farming country; and that was when Bro Abe Gardner told about seeing the first automobile in Brewton; and that was when Old Tyler McIntosh told the one he said Mr. Ike used to laugh himself to tears about, the one about how Calvin Hargroves had made a complete and everlasting, clodhopping fool out of himself the day the first airplane flew over that part of Alabama:

He had left his mule and plow right where they were in the middle of the field when he heard it. And then he looked up and saw it—and struck out across the fence to tell everybody to get ready because the old Ship of Zion was coming. That, of course, was outrageous enough to ruin him for life, but the thing he was never able to live down, the thing that finally drove him north to Cincinnati, Ohio, was the fact that he went running to the whitefolks first.

He spent most of that next year trying to explain that he had only done so because he wanted to find out whether the whitefolks had been reading anything about anything like that in the newspapers, since the only things any of the folks he knew ever read were the Bible, the old Blueback Webster and the *Farmer's Almanac*. But that didn't change anybody's suspicions in the least. Because Calvin Hargroves had started running and yelling about the old Ship of Zion, which was what he really believed it was, which meant he also believed it was Judgment Day so the first thing he should have done was go and get his own family ready to get on board, not the whitefolks.

He could never answer that to anybody's satisfaction and it finally got so that all he would do was hang his head. And then when all of it was finally beginning to die down the whitefolks found out that the Negroes had a big joke about it. And they grabbed it and changed the whole point and started it all over again and it was as if it had just happened.

So finally he had had to give up and move on out of that part of the country and on out of the South. Because when that part got started, every time he went into town at least two or three of them would come up to him or call him over to them and tell him that what he had done proved what a good nigger he was, and he couldn't refuse to take the fifty-cent pieces the rich ones handed him and then the rednecks found out about it and got into it and he also had to pick up the nickles and dimes they threw at him and before long even the little hay-haired, rat-piss-

smelling, barefooted, splotchy-faced, hungry-looking redneck children were throwing pennies at him.

Then he had to come back among homefolks with
everybody knowing about all that and not saying another
word about it anymore because the joke was over and all
that was left of it was the kind of mess the whitefolks
always loved so much. That was when folks woke up one
morning and found out that he had packed up that night
and left without saying anything to anybody. Some years
later they found out that he was living in Cincinnati, and
the last thing anybody had heard was that one of his boys
was working on the lake boats out of Buffalo and another
was a musician in a New York speakeasy.

Then they were talking about the whitefolks and the
days of slavery again and the folks who were there that
night were Aunt Classie Belsaw and Uncle Jim Bob Ewing,
and when they started recollecting life on the old plantations, the Civil War (calling it The Silver War) and Surrender, everybody sat listening as everybody always did
when somebody like that was remembering olden times.

Aunt Classie, who was always dressed in gingham and
an apron and always wore plain-toed, old lady comforter
shoes and either a bonnet or a head-rag, was sitting in the
highbacked cane rocking chair; and everybody knew that
every now and then she was going to say And then
. . . Ole Marster . . . and pause and rock puffing at her clay
pipe; and then say And then Ole Marster say, hum, yes and
then the nigger, huh, huh, huh, yesn Lord. Then she would
rock back and forth puffing and getting the next part together for herself and then say Yes, Lord, again and begin
not at the beginning but with the climax and signification:
And then so here come Ole Marster just a-coming in there,
and then all them other whitefolks they running every-

where like a chicken with his neck wrung and that's when the nigger done figured out something else and biding his time studying about the next chance. That was her way and you knew that she was not ready for anybody else to say anything or ask anything until she finally said So there, by God.

Then Uncle Jim Bob, who was born in slavery, but was freed before he was big enough to realize what it meant to be under the yoke, was talking about being a child during the Silver War and growing up during Reconstruction. He was sitting on the rattan yard chair and he talked with his chin moving up and down against the back of his hand which cushioned it against the top of his Scotch-Irish-Ashanti walking stick. After every three or four words he smacked his lips with great-grandfatherly self-satisfaction as if he were chewing on the curd of wisdom itself while giving you time to let each step of a process become clear before moving on the next. Then to make sure you got the point he would go back over it and condense it: Well, now sir, here's what it all boil down to in a nutshell. The white-folks they always trying to make out like were none of that nothing but just one great big old free nigger mananial mess. Of course they does, but I'm right here to vouch for them and there were so many cunning ones right there in amongst them. Talking about right here in Alabama in Montgomery and all the way up the line to Washington City, D.C., and didn't none of them old Confederate whitefolks understand that many niggers done found out all that about government business and couldn't none of them figure out nothing to do with them but wait until they got them to call the Yankees on back up North and that's when they started whipping them and killing them up right and left while the Yankees off somewhere studying about something else. But that just slowed them down, but it couldn't stop them long as the answer was in the ballot box. So they still had to cheat them away from there and that's how come today we got Poll Tax which ain't nothing but nigger tax spreading like trying to keep up with mooter grass on down to this day and time and that's what I'm talking about when you hear me talking about the young generation coming up now because they the ones got to know what to do because ain't many of us old heads left because who would even nine thought that I would still be here to see Ike Meadows on his cooling board. Who would thought that because he weren't no child and I was along there with his pappy.

Lord, Miss Et, Jesus, Miss Minnie Ridley Stovall said, because they were all thinking about the wake again then, and Miss Liza Jefferson said When the Lord gets ready for you, Jesus, because God knows Et done what she could.

And I knew they were coming to that part again and I was going to have to hear them go all over all of it again detail by detail from the first day the pain struck. Then they were going to repeat what they had seen and heard and said beginning with the time he took to bed and come all the way up to his very last words; and there was nothing you could do but see the room and the bed and him lying there with the window shades drawn, and then you could hear how his breath began to sink and the dry death rattle settling in and see the glassy look come into his eyes and then there was only the feeble movement of his lips saying nothing and his hands trembling and the last gasp and he was gone for ever and ever and ever.

Like I say, Miss Liza Jefferson said, . . .

Thy will be done Jesus, Miss Ina Hopkins said, That's what the good book say, and thy kingdom come.

Well, the Lord blessed him with Et for his wife, Mister

175

Jeff Jefferson put in then, and he blessed him twice with two fine chillun.

Old Skeeter on his way from Detroit, Michigan, too, Mister Horace Upshaw said. That boy love his daddy and he made a fine man. Up there working for old Henry Ford and got three of his own, two boys and a girl.

An Euralee already here all the way from out in Los Angeles, California.

That's what somebody said, Miss Ina Hopkins said.

That's right, honey, Miss Liza Jefferson said then. She here all right. Et sent for her first and she got in here on the Crescent from New Orleans last night. They got her over at Lula Crayton's so she can get some rest for the funeral. That's how come Lula ain't over here tonight.

Well, I can tell you this much, Mister Jeff Jefferson said Et ain't got a thing to worry about with two fine chillun like that.

Old Euralee sure seeing herself some of the world, Mister Horace Upshaw said, Out there working for one of them picture show women and been all across the water with her.

Guess who else Euralee say out there in California working for some of them big moving picture people? Miss Liza Jefferson said. Luvenia Lewis. Euralee say she out there cooking. Say she so fat and fine you wouldn't even know her.

Out there cooking what? Miss Ina Hopkins said. I know when that child was born, and I ain't never heard nobody say she can even string a chicken.

Lord, whitefolks'll eat anything, Jesus, Miss Minnie Ridley Stovall said.

But that's just what I am talking about these children surprising you, Mister Horace Upshaw said. Little devils

176

subject to be hiding a lot more get-up than me and you give them credit for.

Young'uns, Uncle Jim Bob said, chewing and smacking his great-grandfather curd again, ain't never been nobody's fool.

Lord, Uncle Jim Bob, but some of them, Jesus, Miss Minnie Ridley Stovall said. Lord I pray, but some of these we got around here.

I was the only young one still there then. But during the earlier part of the night almost everybody in that part of Gasoline Point had stopped by to sit for awhile and during that time I was out in Stranahan's Lane, and so was Little Buddy and old Cateye Gander Gallagher and so was Estelle Saunders, who was Little Buddy's girl then; and old Gander had his cat eyes on Felisha Coleman; and since Charlene Wingate had gone to spend that summer with her cousins in New York and Deljean McCray had to stay home that night, the one I had was Ella Crenshaw.

It was June and it was warm enough for anybody to be barefooted who wanted to and most of us were and some of the rest of us others took off our sneakers and strung them on the garden gate. There were fireflies blinking in and out of the sunflower clusters along the fence that night and you could hear the guineas roosting in the trees behind Miss Amanda Scott Randolph's cookshop. There was also the smell of dog fennels whenever a breeze had stirred and when you ran down the soft talcum-dry lane the sand dust hung behind you in the moonlight like exhaust pipe fumes.

Some of the others there during that part of the night were Eddie Lee Wilcox, Buddy Baby, and Sister Baby, the Sawyer twins, Martha Ann Pool, Ginny Taylor, Marvin Walker and about ten others plus Nango, Jet, Nerva and Early G. who were there to sing as a junior quartet. At first we were all at the pump shed, which was halfway between the yard where the wake was·and the back of Stranahan's store which was where Stranahan's Lane curved and sloped down into Buckshaw Mill Road. That meant that we were far enough away and that our noise would not disturb the wake; and for a while all we did was sit around swapping riddles and playing ring games. But as far as Little Buddy and I were concerned we were just waiting until Big-toed Cateye could finally get Felisha to say yes.

Then we got everybody to play hide-and-seek because we already knew a good place in the thickets along the ridge of the old Confederate breastworks above the crawfish pond. We had it all figured out and came back in to touch base twice, and then that's where we were until they called everybody into the yard to be served refreshments.

Reverend Wilson Mack Palmer was there then and that was when the quartets sang. It started with Nango, Jet, Nerva and Early G. who represented The Intermediate Banner of Good Hope Baptist Sunday School. Then each one of the others gave two selections, and Gaither Williams, whose brother was Claiborne Williams, the juke joint piano player, came on with the Harmonizers and took his famous bass solo on "Remember Me On Mound Caveree." Then after The Pine Star Four from Pine Hill Chapel finished, everybody who was not going to sit until morning said goodnight and left, and I had to stay because it was Mama's committee's time and Papa and Uncle

178

Jerome were on the waterfront unloading a banana boat that night.

That's why I was still there, and when I woke up and realized where I was I guessed that it must have been three o'clock, so I didn't move. I kept my eyes closed and listened but not because I was eavesdropping, I was really trying to hear the locusts and go back to sleep. When Miss Minnie Ridley Stovall started talking to Mama, I was only listening then because lying with your head in somebody's lap like that, every time the answer came you could feel all of the vibrations even before you heard the sound of her voice.

What I really wanted to do was hear the three o'clock locusts and forget about being at the wake and go back to sleep and be ready to go rambling with Little Buddy in Bay Poplar Woods while everybody else was at the funeral the next afternoon. I wasn't even interested when Miss Liza Jefferson started talking about me; because all she was doing was saying The little man all played out and sleeping like a log, dead to the world from ripping and running with all that friskiness from God knows where, but he sure ain't puny no more. My, they sure do grow. Be done stretched on up here getting all mannish before you know it, Miss Melba. And all Mama did was chuckle and run her hand over my head again and say: He's mama's Little Man out there among them. That's what he is, mama's Little Scootabout Man. I knew all about that kind of talk and I was really trying not to hear it. I was really listening through it and the summertime sound of the swing to the yard crickets and bush locusts, and I was already dozing off again.

So I missed the first part of what Miss Minnie Ridley Stovall said about me this time. What woke me up was Mama responding, and I could tell by the vibrations that she didn't want to have to talk about whatever it was. Then Miss Minnie Ridley Stovall sucked her gold tooth twice as she always did when she was gossiping about something and I knew she was going to say something more, and she did.

Of course me, myself, it an't none of my business, Jesus. Lord knows I know that, Miss Melba. So that's why like I say I ain't never asked you a thing about any of it before, and I don't even know who the one started it. All I know is what everybody keep saying. So I just say to myself, I'm going to ask Miss Melba. That's the only way to set em straight, if you don't mind, Miss Melba.

Folks always running their mouth about something, Mister Horace Upshaw said. If it ain't one thing it's another and if it ain't another it's something else.

It sure God is, Jesus, Miss Minnie Ridley Stovall said.

And don't none of them know the first thing about it, Miss Liza Jefferson said, Not a one.

That's exactly why I said I was going to ask Miss Melba, Miss Minnie Ridley Stovall said. If you don't mind, Miss Melba.

Ask me what? Mama said.

About Edie Bell Boykin, Miss Minnie Ridley Stovall said.

Ask me what about Edie Bell Boykin? Mama said, and the way she said it made me suddenly numb all over.

Some of them saying he really belongs to her, Miss Minnie Ridley Stovall said.

He belong to me, Mama said.

See there, Mister Horace Upshaw said.

But before anybody else could say anything else Mama's stomach was vibrating again and I felt the sound start and heard it go and then it came out through her mouth as words:

She brought him into the world but he just as much mine as my own flesh and blood. I promised her and I promised God.

The Bible speaks of such things, Miss Ina Hopkins said from the swing. And it speaks of rewards, Miss Melba.

I have my reward, Sis Ina, Mama's stomach and voice said against and above my spinning head and ringing ears.

Poor little thing, Miss Minnie Ridley Stovall said. Poor little lamb.

Poor little thing nothing, Miss Liza Jefferson said. He here, aint he, don't care how he got here.

I'm just talking about not knowing your own flesh and blood, Miss Minnie Ridley Stovall said.

I promised her and I promised God, Mama said. *And she promised me and Whit before God.*

I was just wondering about his own daddy that spermed and begot him, Miss Minnie Ridley Stovall said. If it ain't asking too much Miss Melba, and like I already said, God knows it ain't none of my business at all.

That's her secret, Mama said. She didn't tell me nothing about that and I ain't never asked her nothing about it and never intend to and I just wish everybody else would just keep their mouths out of it.

Amen, Miss Liza Jefferson said. Amen.

That's exactly what I tell em Miss Melba, Miss Minnie Ridley Stovall said. That's exactly what I always did say and at least anybody can see the other party wasn't no white man, whoever it was.

That next morning my head had stopped spinning and my ears were not ringing anymore and I was no longer numb, but I didn't want to have to talk to anybody or even be near anybody. Not even Little Buddy Marshall. So I kept to myself all day that day and went to bed early and when I woke up the morning after that I had decided to act as if nothing had happened.

It was not until months later that I finally decided to mention anything about that night to Little Buddy Marshall. But all I said was Man you know something? One time I caught Old Lady Booty Butt Minnie Ridley-butt Stovall trying to gossip some old hearsay stuff about me and Miss Tee. But she don't know I heard her—and Mama and Papa neither.

Which is when Little Buddy Marshall said: Man my mama made me promise her on the Bible I wouldn't never say anything about nothing like that until after you brought it up first. But shoot man you want to know the truth? Shoot man the reason I didn't even need her to make me swear? Because man that's good as giving you the inside claim on old Luzana and old Stagolee and old Gator Gus and them and all that. Because man you welcome to Old Lady Metcalf and all that old school stuff. But shoot man. Goddamn. Not that.

I was never able to bring myself to ask Miss Tee anything at all about what I heard that night at the wake. So I have no way of knowing when and how she learned that I had found out who she really was. But she already knew by the time I finished the Ninth Grade and she also must have assumed that I knew that she knew. Because as pleased as she was to see me come hop-skipping up the steps with my certificate and the top prize, what she said without realizing that she was winking as if for me to remember some secret agreement was But My Mister don't you think we better let Miss Melba always be the one to see things first and then ask her if it's all right to come let Miss Tee be next? And I said I forgot. And when I looked back from the gate she was waving and smiling and there were tears in her eyes.

DATE DUE